"Don't try to

He knelt on the hay beside her. "Wait till help arrives. Your baby is right here. See? Safe."

She reached out and touched the baby's head. "Melody," the woman whispered. "I can't help her right now. Please don't hurt her. She's so little."

Nathan sat back on his heels wondering why this odd woman kept demanding that he not hurt them. What kind of monster would hurt a new mother and her child?

"Her name is Melody?" he asked, trying to make small talk and sound calm. "How old is she?"

"Two weeks yesterday."

"What's your name?"

The woman groaned and pursed her lips. Apparently that was one question she didn't want to answer.

What the hell did he have on his hands? Who was she and where had she come from? That she was running away from something seemed fairly obvious.

★ ★ ★

Dear Reader,

I must've been sitting under my lucky star when I was chosen to write one of the books in the Perfect, Wyoming continuity. Sometimes you just luck out, you know?

What a series this is! Perfect, Wyoming is a nickname for Cold Plains, a town that has been taken over by a cult. The town is now populated with glassy-eyed, beautiful people who are devoted to a charismatic leader. But an evil presence pervades the small town. Children are missing and beautiful women are dying.

Chilling.

The best part for me of writing one of the books in the series is the terrific group of authors who wrote the rest of the books. How could we miss with wonderful authors Marie Ferrarella, Kimberly Van Meter, Jennifer Morey, Loreth Anne White and Carla Cassidy in the line-up?

My book, *Rancher's Perfect Baby Rescue,* is book #2 in the six-book series. It tells the story of a rancher with demons and his call to rescue a single mother on the run. Come along on Nathan and Susannah's thrilling adventure.

Happy reading!

Linda Conrad

LINDA CONRAD

*Rancher's Perfect
Baby Rescue*

ROMANTIC
SUSPENSE

Special thanks and acknowledgment to Linda Conrad for her contribution to the Perfect, Wyoming, miniseries.

Recycling programs
for this product may
not exist in your area.

ISBN-13: 978-0-373-27762-9

RANCHER'S PERFECT BABY RESCUE

www.Harlequin.com

Printed in U.S.A.

Books by Linda Conrad

LINDA CONRAD

When asked about her favorite things, Linda Conrad lists a longtime love affair with her husband, her sweetheart of a dog named KiKi and a sunny afternoon with nothing to do but read a good book. Inspired by generations of storytellers in her family and pleased to have many happy readers' comments, Linda continues creating her own sensuous and suspenseful stories about compelling characters finding love.

A bestselling author of more than twenty-five books, Linda has received numerous industry awards, among them the National Reader's Choice Award, the Maggie, the Write Touch Reader's Award and the *RT Book Reviews* Reviewers' Choice Award. To contact Linda, to read more about her books or to sign up for her newsletter and/or contests, go to her website, www.lindaconrad.com.

To Patience Bloom and Shana Smith with my thanks for making this book the best it could be.

Chapter 1

"Shush, baby. Please. They mustn't hear us."

Susannah Paul ducked through the cold darkness, dodging tree limbs and praying that her two-week-old little girl would not cry out. Howling winds rustled through the black-as-night woods, sending her scurrying.

Away. If she could fly, high above the rocky, tangled terrain, the two of them would be hundreds of miles away from the town of Cold Plains and its potential dangers. It seemed as if she and the baby had been on the run for hours. Day had become night, and it was harder than ever trying to make her way through the dense forest.

She had no idea how long it had been since she'd bid goodbye to her friend May Frommer and dashed into the woods in broad daylight, but she couldn't stop now—not until she was sure they would not be found.

The baby in the carrier at her breast whimpered low, her cries so pitiful and weak that Susannah's heart winced. *We'll stop soon, my darling Melody. Mommy will find safety, I promise. I know you're hungry.*

Frustrated to the point of blindness by not being able to slow her steps long enough to feed her child, Susannah barged into a gully and practically tripped over fallen tree limbs in her way. Breathing heavily, she scolded herself for not paying closer attention. It would never do for her to fall. She couldn't while carrying her baby and with the heavy pack of their meager belongings on her back.

At the far side of the gully, the moon broke through heavy foliage and lit her surroundings just enough for her to get her bearings. It was infinitely harder to find her way in the pitch darkness than earlier that morning when she'd gotten directions.

She needed to stop for a moment. They both required water, a little breather.

Leaning against the thick trunk of a tall pine, she pulled a baby bottle from her coat pocket and placed it against her child's lips. "Please drink, sweetheart," she whispered.

Baby Melody seemed drugged and had little interest in the bottle she hadn't learned to use even in the best of surroundings. "I know. You want Mama's milk. But we can't stop that long right now."

Susannah placed a couple of drops of the liquid against the child's mouth, hoping some would spill inside, then she pulled off the nipple and drank a couple of swallows herself. Stale. She didn't blame her child for not being interested in water that tasted old, but her baby needed liquid. It had been several hours since she'd halted their escape long enough to breast-feed.

Did she dare try it now? While they were stopped for the moment, Susannah quieted her breathing and listened for any sign that their pursuers were closing in. She heard leaves rustling in the wind but nothing that sounded like men crashing through the forest after them.

How had she gotten into this position in the first place? Everything that had once been so clean and good had suddenly turned so rotten and dangerous. It didn't seem fair.

But most of her life hadn't been fair, either, she realized. She'd been hoping that the new circumstances and pleasant people she'd found in Cold Plains would do the trick and change her life around—for Melody's sake, if not for hers.

The baby didn't deserve to start out her life this way. She hadn't done anything wrong. Susannah refused to allow this kind of prejudice against her child. Melody was not going to suffer the fate she had.

A single tear rolled from the edge of her eye, but Susannah couldn't cry. She couldn't afford to waste the bodily fluids. Biting her cheek to make the tears stop, she tried thinking back to how happy she'd been on the day Melody was born.

That morning she'd walked twelve blocks to the other edge of town, already in labor but determined to reach her new friend's cottage before the birth. May Frommer was one of the kindest people Susannah had ever met—well, next to Samuel Grayson, that was. And May had been waiting with open arms.

Lately Samuel had been too busy selling his health-giving waters and with his duties as leader of the Devotees to spend much time with her. On the other hand,

May was the town's midwife, not one of the Devotees but someone who'd lived in Cold Plains all her life.

May had been secretly helping with her pregnancy for months. To be sure, Susannah had also gone to the special parenting classes given by the Devotees. Their classes were extremely helpful for a woman who knew absolutely nothing about being a mother. Her own mother had not been much of an example.

But when it came right down to it, Susannah felt a bit nervous about using the Devotees' tiny urgent-care facility for regular maternity checkups. She wasn't too sure why she felt that way. After all, she'd been ready to turn over the rest of her life to the Devotees. Their facility and most of the town for that matter was brand-new and sparkling clean, and everyone was so pleasant. But she just wasn't comfortable at their urgent care. And though she'd heard a new doctor had also recently come to town and opened his own office, May had already volunteered weeks ago, and Susannah was happy it turned out so well.

The two of them developed a great relationship in the couple of months they'd known each other. They were like sisters almost. May even invited her to have the baby at her cottage instead of Susannah's tiny room at the boardinghouse in town.

For two weeks after Melody's birth, she and the baby had stayed at May's while she learned how to breast-feed and care for a tiny infant. Everything seemed nearly perfect...until May began putting thoughts into her head.

And then this morning...

Clouds suddenly covered the moon, and Susannah heard an odd noise. Turning her head to the sound, she jolted at the sight of gleaming yellow eyes staring at her from out of the bushes. Night creatures. Were they dangerous? Visions of wolves came to mind, sending chills down her spine.

It was time to leave.

But which way? She knew she couldn't travel much longer without resting, and the baby desperately needed feeding. But she was becoming turned around in the darkness. How far had they come?

Taking a deep breath, Susannah made a best guess at the right direction and started out through the forest again. Within seconds, the moonlight broke through clouds and canopy, leading her way. She found what looked like a path. Well, maybe it was not a real path but at least a wide place where the brush was not so heavy and the ground seemed level. She rejoiced and followed along. Positive she was at least not headed back toward town, she picked up her pace and hoped to quickly find the highway she'd been seeking all day.

Another ten minutes went by until she came upon a fence. It wasn't much of a fence, just a few wires strung together, but it gave her hope. There was hope for civilization ahead.

She bowed her head to go under one high wire while stepping over the lowest one. Before long, she came to the realization that a fence could be very bad news. What if she'd gotten turned around worse than she'd thought and the fence belonged to the Devotees? They did own property, like the creek and a few isolated houses, which backed up to these same woods. This fence could be at the edge of their property.

She couldn't guess how many miles she might have traveled today. It was difficult going, fighting her way through the woods with an infant. But she was determined to keep moving ahead. There could be no going back.

As she kept walking and left the fence behind, the woods became less and less dense. Through the trees, she began catching glimpses of structures in the moonlight up ahead—buildings...civilization...people.

She hesitated again, unsure about this. Maybe it was a bad idea to barge in on a stranger, one who could likely be another Devotee.

Gritting her teeth, she walked on in fear. In moments, she came to a clear area surrounding what looked like farm buildings: big barns and sheds. Bright floodlights blazed from every corner of each building, but it seemed no one was around. She hadn't heard of the Devotees owning any ranch or farm.

Listening closely, she couldn't hear a sound except the same crickets and night noises she had been hearing since sunset. Maybe everyone had gone to bed.

She started trembling. The air felt chilly in the woods at night, and spring in Wyoming was known for its cold nights and warm days. But she felt sure her trembling must be coming more from fear than from the weather.

Still, she and Melody needed to get in out of the elements and rest—right now.

She held her breath and prayed again that the baby would sleep quietly through the next few minutes; she gingerly tiptoed over the short grasses and bare dirt. Fortunately, the nearest building wasn't too far from the fence.

She noticed a small door at the back of the huge barnlike structure. Mentally crossing her fingers, she tried the latch. It was open. With another deep breath and with a tiny protest of the hinges, she and Melody were safely inside.

Susannah had to wait a few minutes for her eyes to adjust to the lower lighting, but once they did, she moved farther into the barn. As she carefully looked around, she decided this place must be used for storage. Near the back door, saddles and tools were strewn across worktables, and all kinds of ropes and equipment hung on the walls.

Walking silently along a wide aisle, she checked right and left. Nothing; there was no sign of human life. As she took a deep breath, she smelled the scent of hay. She knew it must be hay because it smelled a little bit like new-mown grass, only stronger.

Susannah turned onto the center aisle and moved past a wooden half wall to find a large room full of bales of hay. One of the bales nearby was broken open and had spilled out in a blanket of hay on the barn floor.

Just at that point, her knees gave out and she sank into the soft hay. This was as far as she could go for now. Surely it wouldn't hurt anything to stay here for a few hours—just long enough to feed the baby, have the last protein bar and maybe catch a little sleep.

She pulled the pack off her back and leaned against it for support as the baby began to stir. "You've been so good, my love. It's time for us to eat now. You first."

Peeling the carrier cover back, she found Melody making sucking motions with her eyes closed. Trying to wake her enough to eat, she tapped lightly on her cheek. "Come on, baby, don't give up. It's finally your time."

After inching her child out of the carrier and into her lap, Susannah checked on her diaper. It was dry, and that could not be a good thing. Melody must not be getting enough fluids.

Peering through the low lighting at her beautiful child, she repeated in her mind what she knew for certain—Melody was perfect. The baby had all her toes and fingers. Susannah had certainly counted them enough times since her birth. And a soft cap of baby fuzz covered her perfectly shaped little head. Big blue eyes, which may or may not change later, stared at the world full of curiosity and followed things as they moved in front of her face. She was perfect.

So, no, the large raspberry-colored birthmark covering her ear and halfway down her neck did not detract from the baby's perfection in any way. It did not!

As she settled Melody at her breast, Susannah tried to relax the way May had shown her. She chewed the protein bar and thought back to a few days after the baby was born. She'd been so enthralled with the miracle of her child's birth that she hadn't noticed the birthmark—not at all.

Then, as May was showing her how to give a real squirming baby a bath, she'd mentioned it for the first time. "The color and the mark itself will probably fade over time. I wouldn't worry about it affecting her life in the future. It's just now that concerns me."

That remark had thrown Susannah a curveball. "How can a birthmark hurt her? I don't understand. Can it make her sick?"

May tested the bathwater and nodded that it was the right temperature. "The mark has nothing to do with her health. But…"

"But what?" Susannah held her daughter in the cradle of her forearm and dunked her body into the water.

"I'm afraid it qualifies her as imperfect in some people's eyes. And that scares me."

Susannah began fighting panic. "Why? What are you talking about?"

"Think about it," May said as she gently wiped a soft, wet cloth across the baby's chest. "When have you ever seen a child, or anyone for that matter, in Cold Plains who wasn't perfect?"

She thought about it for a moment. "Everyone in Cold Plains is beautiful—and perfect. I can't think of one person I've seen in a wheelchair or using a cane. Even the elderly are robust and take power walks in the park. I've noticed all the beautiful people but never considered that significant. What do you believe it means?"

May tenderly rubbed the baby's toes and fingers. "I've been midwife in this area for years—long before Samuel Grayson and the Devotees came to town and disrupted everything. Take my word for it, not all babies born in this town are absolutely perfect. You see every kind of birth defect here that you see anywhere else."

Susannah's hands began to shake. "What happens to those babies? Where do they go?"

"Here, let me help you." May slid her hand under Susannah's and pulled the baby from the water.

Next, she laid the child down on a soft towel and showed Susannah how to pat her dry. "There're lots of wild rumors about what happens to the babies. One I heard suggests the imperfect little ones are taken out of town and given to new parents who can handle the defect."

When Susannah gasped her horror, May pursed her lips and handed over a dry and happy Melody. "Another rumor is even worse. I heard there's a secret room located under the community-center complex where everyone who's not perfect is, well, maybe not in prison but out of sight."

Susannah cradled her baby. "You're kidding, right? The Devotees aren't like that. They're kind and generous, and they really care about people. It's impossible."

Shrugging a shoulder, May asked, "What's the one thing you like best about the Devotees?"

"That's easy. The 'Being the Best You' seminars Samuel gives every evening. They're wonderful. He actually makes me think I can do the things I never thought I could."

"In other words, those seminars make you believe you can be perfect. You're already beautiful on the outside, but you think becoming a Devotee will make you beautiful on the inside, too?"

"Well…" Not when May put it that way. "I guess not."

"But being perfect is important to Samuel and his Devotees. Would you agree?"

"I suppose."

May give her a wry smile. "It's time for another breast-feeding lesson. Why don't you just think over what we've talked about? You have a few days yet before you need to take the baby to town and go back to the Devotees."

Susannah had thought about it. The idea grew in her mind until she could think of nothing else. Finally, she told May that she didn't want to take any chances with her baby but didn't know what else to do. She loved the Devotees and loved the town of Cold Plains.

Torn, Susannah went through the next few days in a haze until one morning when one of Samuel's friends, a nice man by the name of Jonathan Miller, called May looking for Susannah.

He told May that he'd heard a rumor that Susannah had already given birth, and the Devotees were eager to welcome the new mom and baby back into their midst. They stood ready to offer her anything she might need.

May hung up, shaking her head. "This is trouble. I told him you weren't here, but I bet he comes here to look for you later today. It's time for a decision."

Suddenly terrified, Susannah gulped down her panic. "We have to leave. Now. This morning. Help me, May. I don't know where to go or what to do. But they can't find Melody here. We can't let that happen."

May took a breath and nodded her agreement. "Okay. Let's get cracking. I can lend you a carrier and a backpack—and the money for a bus from the highway to Laramie. You'll find help in Laramie. I'll give you a few numbers to call."

After they had packed up the bag, Susannah remembered the one missing piece of their plan. "How will the baby and I get to the highway bus stop?"

"I can drive—" May stopped talking when the sound of a car turning into her long driveway came through the trees. "Oh, Lord. They're here. You'll have to walk. Out the back way through the woods. Quick. Here's a map and general directions. Don't let them spot you."

Susannah put the baby in the carrier and hurried to slide the backpack over her shoulders. She tore out the back door of May's house at a dead run and never turned around.

Tired and exasperated with his family, Nathan Pierce rolled his tight muscles as he strolled across the barnyard toward the foreman's quarters. It was almost dawn, and he'd had maybe two hours of sleep last night. And now he was out here looking for the ranch foreman to issue orders for the day before he could even start breakfast.

Reminding himself for the fiftieth time in the past two days that he loved his family's ranch enough to stick around when things got rough, Nathan sighed and whistled for the dogs. While he was out this far, he might as well make sure they were fed and groomed.

With one whistle, old Joey came running, barking and bouncing in the morning's gray light. The shepherd was a longtime favorite. But where were the rest of the hounds?

The care of these dogs was the only thing he expected his brother to handle. Was even that too much to ask of the man who actually owned the whole place?

Sighing with frustration, Nathan thought back to how he'd gotten in this position. His mother's father, the one who'd built this ranch from a humble few acres into a grand showplace, died eight years ago. He had loved his granddaddy dearly, but every day since he'd passed away, Nathan had cussed out the old man for leaving the ranch to his oldest grandchild.

What the hell had Isaac been thinking? Nathan might've understood if his grandfather had bequeathed the place to his son-in-law, Nathan's father, Evan. But Evan and Isaac had never agreed on anything—least of all on the management of the land. So Nathan's older brother, Derek, ended up with everything.

Not that Derek cared one way or the other. Right after the reading of the will, his brother had turned over management of the place to their father—against all his grandfather's wishes.

Where were those dogs? Nathan whistled again and

then listened. He heard Buck the coonhound baying from somewhere nearby. Buck never bayed like that unless he had a critter cornered.

Hell. It was just another chore that would have to be attended to before he could start his day.

Nathan strode forcefully toward the dogs' commotion, wondering if he would need a rifle to dispatch whatever kind of critter could have wandered into one of the barns. He hated the thought of killing a hapless wild animal and decided to try shooing whatever it was back out into the woods without deadly force. He just hoped the damned thing wasn't a skunk.

By the time he reached the dogs, his ranch foreman was coming from around the other side of the barn with a rifle already in hand.

"Hold it, Mac. Take charge of the dogs, and let me see what we've got cornered before we go tearing in, guns blazing."

"Okay, boss. It's your skin." With a grin, Mac grabbed the three dogs by their collars and held tight.

Nathan shook his head and entered the largest hay barn. Was he being foolish to come unprotected? Stopping right inside the door to pick up a pitchfork, he cautiously walked down the long center aisle while being careful to check both right and left among the huge stored hay bales.

Toward the end of the aisle, right before the entrance to the tool storage area, Nathan heard a strange noise. He stopped and listened intently. What was that sound? It wasn't like any animal he'd ever encountered. Then after a few seconds he took that sentiment back.

The noise sounded for all the world like the mewling cries of a newborn kitten. Jeez. The dogs were going nuts over a new litter of kittens?

Just in case he was wrong, Nathan hefted the pitchfork in both hands and crept quietly around the half wall on his way to the main storage room and the cries.

What he saw on the other side of the wall stopped him cold—not kittens. There, hunkered down in the hay, was a gorgeous woman cradling a fussy newborn infant in her arms.

After finding his voice, he cleared his throat and tried to calm her. "Uh, excuse me. Miss. Um. Mrs..."

The woman blinked her eyes and then jolted straight up, pointing at the pitchfork. "Oh, don't hurt us. Who are you? I..." Her eyes rolled back in her head, and she collapsed into the hay.

Worried about the infant's safety, Nathan dropped the fork and swooped up the child before it fell out of its mother's arms.

What the devil had he gotten himself into now?

Chapter 2

Susannah blinked open her eyes and found the tall, slightly scary man bending over her with Melody in his arms.

Frightened but ready to fight like a tiger for her child, she came up swinging. "Give her to me!"

"Whoa," he said as he backed away. "Hold on there. I'm not trying to hurt you or your baby. You fainted. I was worried about you both. Are you all right?"

"I…" Light-headedness made her unsure of herself. "Um. I guess I'm okay. It's been a while since I've eaten. Maybe that's the problem.

"Please give me the baby." She tried to stand, and the whole world tilted.

Reaching out, she found a post that she could hang on to while she waited for the room to quit spinning. Her stomach churned as she felt the blood drain from her face.

"Look, you don't seem too steady. Maybe I should keep your child until you get your feet under you."

She plopped back down on the hay. "I guess you're right. Just give me a minute."

"Stay right where you are. I'll call for help." He turned and disappeared beyond the half wall.

Oh, no. He was either calling the cops to come arrest her for trespassing or he was calling the Devotees to pick up their runaways.

As usual, she'd made a hash out of May's very good plan. How could she get out of this sticky situation? Oh, yeah, if all else failed, she could lie.

Nathan was halfway to the front of the barn before he realized he still had the baby in his arms. He hesitated and looked down at her.

Tiny, the little babe couldn't possibly be more than a few days old. And the baby was quiet. Since he'd been holding her, she hadn't cried once.

In fact, this child seemed too quiet.

Looking her over, he couldn't find anything obviously wrong—no cuts or bruises. Her color was a little off. She seemed drugged.

His niece had never been so quiet when she was this age. Of course his niece—well, Sara had always been different than most. Logically, he knew that. And though she was seven now, he figured he'd end up comparing her to every baby he met from now on.

"What'd you find, boss?" Mac stood at the front of the barn, peering toward the bundle he carried in his hands as if trying to decide what kind of dangerous critter they'd discovered.

Walking toward his foreman, Nathan shook his head. "Not a critter. But we need help. Put the dogs up and call the house. See if Maria or Kathryn can get down here right away. Tell whoever to bring a bottle of water."

Mac wrinkled up his forehead. "What the hell?"

"Put the dogs in the pen, Mac. I don't want one of them jumping up to see what I've got."

"Okay. Right away." Mac turned and started off toward the dogs' pen.

"And make that call!"

Nathan turned around and headed back toward the mother. He didn't want to venture too much farther while carrying this small child. Poor little baby. When he'd first seen the two of them huddled in the hay, they'd looked like two lost angels—both gorgeous and wide-eyed.

The mother was one of the most striking women he'd ever seen, with her long, dark hair and porcelain skin. Stunning, even though her eyes had been filled with fright, she looked like a strong wind could blow her over.

Now that he'd had a chance to look closer at the child, however, he noticed a wide reddish mark on the side of her head and neck. She was still a beauty. Almost a spitting image of her mother.

"Don't worry, little one," he whispered. "I've got you now. I won't let anything happen to you or your mom."

The baby never stirred as he carried her back to where her mother waited. When he ducked around the half wall, the woman tried to stand again. She wobbled and went down on her backside

"Don't try to move." He knelt on the hay beside her. "Wait till help arrives. One of the women will be out shortly. Your baby is right here. See? Safe."

She reached out and touched the baby's head. "Melody." Closing her eyes, the woman whispered through a sigh, "I can't help her right now. Please don't hurt her. She's so little."

Nathan sat back on his heels, wondering why this odd woman kept demanding that he not hurt them. What kind of monster would hurt a new mother and her child?

"Her name is Melody?" he asked, trying to make small talk and sound calm. "Pretty. How old is she?" He wanted to keep the woman talking so he could be sure she hadn't passed out.

"Two weeks yesterday."

"What's your name?"

The woman groaned and pursed her lips. Apparently that was one question she didn't want to answer. What the hell did he have on his hands? Who was she, and where had she come from? That she was running away from something seemed fairly obvious.

"You needed help, Nathan?" Maria, his family's housekeeper, peered around the half wall. "Oh, my goodness. What on earth?" She made short shrift of the few feet between them.

"You bring the water with you?" He glanced over at Maria and saw the bottle in her hands. "Give this young woman a drink and then take the baby, please."

Maria crouched to help the stranger take a sip of water. "Where'd you come from, Mrs.?"

The woman drank a few sips and then widened her eyes to stare at Maria. "Help my baby." She grabbed hold of her arm in a deathlike grip. "Melody needs water, too, but I don't know how to make her drink."

Maria pulled her arm free and stood, then took the child from his hands. "Ah, a tiny one. You leave her to me, ma'am. I'll have her taking water in no time."

Maria glanced up at him. "This child needs warmth and the comfort of the main house."

He nodded at his housekeeper. "Thanks. I think I can carry the mother if you've got a handle on the baby."

"Yes, sir." Maria reached over and picked up the woman's backpack with her free hand. "Looks like the pack is probably being used for baby's things. I can carry it, too." She walked away, still making cooing noises at the child.

Bending to scoop the stranger off the floor, Nathan thought he might have trouble hefting her. She jolted, and he could see her holding her breath. But actually her body came up in his arms almost too easily.

"You hardly weigh a thing," he said while he marched toward the barnyard.

"I can walk. You don't have to carry me."

"Last time I saw you trying to stand you weren't too steady. I think this is the safest way for now."

"We're going to your house? How far is it?"

"Not far. We'll be there in a few minutes."

"Do you own this farm?"

Tightening his grip on her, he exhaled and answered the slightly annoying question. "It's a ranch. And my family owns it. For a trespasser, you're just full of questions, aren't you?"

She shut her mouth and narrowed it in a tight line.

"I'm Nathan Pierce, and I've answered all your questions. How about answering another of mine? What's your name?"

Suddenly she looked terrified again. "Susannah. Susannah Paul."

Her big eyes were pleading with him for some kind of mercy. And he didn't have a clue what it was all about.

"That's better. Nice name. And Melody is your baby. Where's her father?"

"I really don't know. He's not around. We weren't married, and he didn't much want a baby."

Her answer had come quick. Apparently the fact that she was on her own wasn't the biggest problem. Something else must be frightening her.

He decided to give her a little time to rest before he questioned her further. Badgering new mothers for answers was not his style—especially ones as beautiful and fragile as this one.

He barged into the kitchen with her in his arms and found a small crowd around the table. The baby was the center of attention.

Maria looked over as they came near. "She's taking a little water, ma'am. Is she on formula? I couldn't find any in her bag."

"I'm breast-feeding." Susannah glared up at him. "If you'll kindly put me down now, I need to take care of my daughter."

"Here? In the kitchen?"

Maria answered for her. "Don't be absurd, Nathan. Carry the mama into your bedroom. It's the closest. And make her comfy. I'll bring the baby along in a moment."

His room? That was the last place he wanted to take this woman. But what did he know about tiny babies? Shutting his mouth, he dutifully did as requested.

How was it that he'd volunteered for this again?

He kicked open the door to his room, and a sudden flash of memory came back to kick him in the gut. Once before he'd carried a woman across the threshold of this room. That time things had not worked out well at all.

But this was different. This woman was not planning on staying.

At least he thought not. On the other hand, his body seemed suddenly to want an entirely different and completely inappropriate plan.

The windows were open, and fresh air filled the room with smells of spring—and maybe a little hint of cattle. It was not unpleasant to him; in fact, it was so ingrained in his life he hardly noticed anymore. But he didn't have any idea what she would think of any of it—smells, cattle, ranch, him.

"The chair or the bed?" He really wanted her to opt for the chair but thought he'd better give her the choice.

"I'm afraid if I lie down I'll fall sound asleep and Melody will never get fed. The chair, please."

He eased her into his reading chair and fluffed the pillow at her back. "This going to be okay?"

"Fine, thanks. It's really nice of you to offer your own room."

The offer had been more of a shanghai. "Later… when you've rested some, we need to talk. My hospitality for your answers. Seems only fair." He stood aside, wondering how fast he could disappear when the baby arrived.

"Fair? Yes, all right. Later."

Maria arrived carrying the baby, and he backed out of his room at a world-record-setting pace. His mind was reeling not only with questions about these two lost souls, like where they came from and why they were running. But another question was why for the first time in nearly four years his libido was reacting to the mere sight and touch of a very attractive but totally unavailable woman.

* * *

Susannah opened her lids, pulling herself from a sound sleep, and for the second time today, she stared up into Nathan's sky-blue eyes. "I must've fallen asleep."

He nodded and sat opposite her on the edge of the bed. "Maria tells me after the baby was fed you had a bite to eat, too, and a little nap. She's looking for something to use as a cradle so she can offer you the chance to clean up and take a shower."

Leaning on his knees, he folded his hands between them and gazed over at her with questions in those terribly sexy eyes. "Feeling well enough for our talk now?"

"I guess." Not really. She would much rather ask questions of her own, like whether or not anyone on the ranch was a Devotee and how far it was from here to the highway bus stop.

"I need to know who you're running from." He raised his eyebrows as if encouraging her to tell him everything.

When she didn't answer, he volunteered a couple of possibilities of his own. "I guess you might be running from some kind of lawman. Did you bug out on the hospital maternity bill? Or maybe you're running from the baby's father? Maria tells me you've got a few cuts and scratches she'd like to tend. You get those from some bastard?"

She hesitated, trying to decide what to say.

"If it's the law that's chasing you, I have to know." He looked so sincere and serious; she wanted to blurt out the whole story. "I'll want to call the Cold Plains police chief. I'm sorry, but I can't harbor any criminals on the ranch. This is a law-abiding place."

She couldn't let him call the Cold Plains police. That was the last thing she needed.

Deciding to go with a half-truth, she said, "The baby's father got angry. He pushed me onto a bus heading east and said he never wanted to see us again. Then when the money almost ran out, the bus dropped us off. Melody and I got turned around, and we've been wandering in the woods looking for someone to help."

Nathan bit his lip as if trying to decide about her story. "So you're saying you walked into the forest on your own? No one chased you in?"

Well, it was half-true. "Yes. That's right. And I kept getting scratched up by all the branches and dead tree limbs. But the baby is safe."

"Uh-huh." He didn't look too convinced. "Okay, then. Where are you from? You have any other family we can contact for help?"

"We're not from anywhere. We—the baby's father and I—were just moving around the country. He… he's a traveling salesman kind of guy." This was pretty much all true.

"And there's no one else?"

"No one." If you took his question literally, she'd just lied. But in her mind and heart there was no one else—at least no one who would care to hear from her under any circumstances, especially not if she needed help.

Nathan stared down at the carpet, and she couldn't tell what he was thinking. All she really wanted was a chance to rest the baby for a few hours and then get directions to the bus.

A knock sounded against the open door. "Nathan?" Maria stuck her head in the room. "Can I come in?"

Maria had told her she was the Pierce family housekeeper. But Susannah had been surprised by that and asked why Maria spoke to Nathan in a manner more like a mother or older sister than an employee. It seemed Maria had been with the family since Nathan's mother died when he was only twelve. She thought of him and his brother as her family now.

"What's up?" Nathan stood when Maria entered.

"I've rigged up a basket for the baby. I can bring the basket in here so Susannah can watch her and still take a nap and grab a shower while the baby naps, if that's all right with you."

"I need to go back to work this afternoon anyhow. Bring it on in."

Maria nodded, then stopped to add something else. "Before you head out, will you make a stop at the front porch? A couple of men who say they're from Cold Plains are waiting to talk to you."

Susannah's veins froze, and the hairs on the back of her neck stood on end. Oh, no. After all she'd been through, they were going to capture her and Melody now?

"Did they say what they wanted?" Nathan didn't look particularly pleased.

Susannah had heard rumors amongst the Devotees that some of the locals hadn't cared for them coming to their town and taking over. Maybe this was proof it was true.

Maria also wrinkled her face as if she'd tasted something sour. "You know I don't talk to none of them Devotees unless I have to. They give me the creeps." She turned and left the room.

Nathan followed Maria's footsteps, also heading for the bedroom door. "You two have a nice rest this afternoon," he said over his shoulder. "We'll talk again."

"Wait." She had to say something to save Melody.

He swung back and stood waiting for her to speak.

"Don't turn us in to the Devotees. Please, Nathan. I beg you for Melody's sake." The tears welled up, and the lump in her throat nearly choked the life right out of her.

Standing there staring at her, his jaw turned hard and his eyes went cold. "So there's a different story you want to give me now?"

"Yes. Yes. Anything. Just please don't tell them we're here."

Nathan stormed out of the room, madder than spit. He should've known—just another beautiful woman who lied. What the hell was the matter with him? Didn't he ever learn?

He'd known her story sounded wrong, but those big hazel eyes had taken him in.

Susannah would have to wait. He had a lot to say to her. But in the meantime, he wanted those frigging Devotee devils the hell off his property.

He hit the front porch ready to go off on them like a rocket. "What do you want?"

The two men turned to his voice. Son of a bitch! One of these dudes was Jonathan Miller, who was absolutely the last man on earth he ever wanted to see again.

"Hello, Nathan." Jonathan's smile was greasy, which went perfectly with his hair. "Sorry to bother you. We were waiting to see your father. Is he in?"

Just the sound of his voice set Nathan's nerves on edge. "No. He's gone to Cheyenne to a breeders' auction. I asked you what you want."

If the Devotees thought they could get around him

every time by going to his father, they were in for a big surprise.

"No sense being hostile." Jonathan's voice was smooth—too smooth. "The problems between us were over years ago. Things have changed. I'm the vice-mayor of Cold Plains now. We're neighbors, Nathan. We want to be good neighbors and friends."

He gritted his teeth and glared at the man. "What part of 'what do you want?' don't you understand? I'm busy, Miller. Say whatever it is and get off our land."

Miller threw a quick glance at the other man, and a chill went up Nathan's spine. The guy had perfect hair, perfect clothes, a perfectly nonthreatening stance and glassy but eerily perfect crystal-blue eyes.

Damned Devotees. Maria was right. They gave him the creeps.

"We're just here asking for a small favor." Jonathan sounded earnest. "Nothing that should upset you. One of our members has disappeared, and we were hoping you would let us look around. We're worried about her."

"What's this person look like?"

"She's in her late twenties with long brown hair. Nine months pregnant, she's within days of having a child. In fact, the birth may have already taken place, and that means there're two of our people who could need help. We're planning on forming a formal search party in the morning."

"Don't bother searching the ranch." Nathan practically spat at the fool. "We'll keep an eye out. If anyone here runs across something odd, I'll be sure to give you a call." The Devotees could rot in hell before he ever lifted one finger to help them.

"But…" Jonathan acted like he seldom was refused anything.

Too bad. "I got your message. Now leave."

"You're not being very neighborly, Nathan. We only wanted…"

"Listen, Miller. If I see any of your people on our property, I'll shoot first and ask questions later." He folded his arms over his chest and took a threatening step forward. "Get out. And don't come back."

The two men turned and walked toward their car without another word. But Nathan had a feeling they weren't about to give up.

He'd call Mac in another minute to escort these two bums off the property. He didn't trust them. In fact, he seldom trusted anyone anymore. It was a hard-learned lesson, one he thought he'd learned well.

So why had one pretty woman who looked lost and alone been able to get under his skin so quickly? Ah, hell.

Regardless, he wanted that Devotee and her child off his ranch and out of his life today.

Chapter 3

Dressed in a borrowed robe while Maria washed her clothes and tried to mend the tears, Susannah awoke from a two-hour nap when a loud knock rapped on the bedroom door. Without waiting for an answer, Nathan banged the door open and came right inside.

"Shush," she told him. "The baby's still sleeping."

He threw a guarded glance toward the basket sitting on his wide dresser top. "I see," he said in a stage whisper. "But we're going to have that talk now."

His face was a mask of stern consternation—big trouble. However, she wouldn't let him run over her. She'd done enough of that in her life. *This time,* her child was what mattered most.

Pulling the robe tighter around her, she carefully sat in the easy chair. "Talk, then. But quietly please."

"I'm not talking. You are. Why'd you lie? And if you're in with those damned Devotees, why didn't you want them to find you?"

She could see the veins sticking out on his temple as his jaw tightened. He was furious. Her hands started shaking. She didn't deal well with anger...never had.

Taking a deep breath, she tried to find a way to explain without making him madder. "Please calm down, Nathan. I'll tell you the truth, why we left Cold Plains, and then Melody and I will leave the ranch. I promise I wasn't trying to take anything from you. We just needed to rest. We were lost. Really."

He drew a breath, too, sat at the edge of the bed like he had earlier and let his mouth relax. "Go on."

"The part about my boyfriend kicking me to the curb when he learned about the baby is true. He did put me on the bus. But that was six months ago. When I ran out of money in the middle of nowhere, I thought I would end up as a street person."

"While expecting a baby?"

"Yeah, that's not such a great picture, is it? The thought scared me to death. But I got lucky for once when Samuel Grayson found me and brought me back to Cold Plains. He made a place for me. He gave me a job and somewhere to live. I'd never been treated so well in my entire life."

Nathan's expression turned hard again. "I can understand that he became like your safety net. I guess you had no choice. But why'd you stay?"

"Seriously? Have you seen the place recently? Everything is wonderful and clean. I'd never lived anywhere as colorful or where the people are so kind to perfect strangers. My life had been full of lots of gray and mostly rude people up to then. I loved it there."

"Did you...did you become one of them?"

"Well, if you mean, did I take their seminars and try my best to be like them? You bet I did. Samuel Grayson is the most amazing person I've ever met. He can make you feel, well, like you're somebody."

A tick appeared at the side of Nathan's mouth when she'd mentioned Samuel. "If you love him and his kind so much, why'd you leave?"

All of a sudden it occurred to her what she'd been feeling during this whole conversation—trust…for Nathan. She barely knew the man but felt sure he would not hurt her or turn her over to the Devotees if she told the whole truth. It was weird to trust someone this quickly, but she went with it.

"Melody. She's the reason we left." Her eyes started to fill again, but she fought the waterworks. "My friend, the midwife named May Frommer, told me all about the rumors and made me see the light. She helped us get away."

"I know May. She's a local. What rumors?"

"About how babies who aren't perfect don't last long in Cold Plains. Look at Melody. She's wonderful and I love her beyond measure, but she isn't perfect."

Sniffling again, she tried to steady her voice. "Have you heard the rumor that Devotees may be stealing children who aren't perfect and selling them? May says so. May also mentioned a basement place where anybody who isn't totally perfect is kept hidden. Do you think that's true?"

"I'd believe anything about those creeps. But are you telling me that because your daughter has a simple birthmark you think she's less than perfect?"

"Not me. I think she's terrific. But, well, I couldn't take a chance that the rumors are true. Could I?"

"Suppose not. So you've given up on Samuel Grayson and his philosophy, then?"

"Oh, no. I'm sure Samuel can't know about any of

this. It must be a few bad people in the Devotees who are using the group as a cover for doing terrible things. And, besides, what's wrong with believing you can become the best you?"

Nathan stood and started pacing the room. "How soon can you get the baby ready to leave? I want you out of here by nightfall."

The bedroom door opened wider at that moment, and Maria stepped into the room. "I heard that, Nathan. What's wrong with you? These two can't leave the ranch yet. Where're your manners? The child is still not healthy. Something's wrong with her, and she needs a doctor. And also there's at least one cut on Susannah that requires stitching."

Nathan ran his hands through his hair. "Hell. Why can't you sew her up? You take care of the rest of us and our little cuts and bumps on the ranch just fine."

"Nothing I've tried has helped the baby. She needs a doctor."

"Who're we gonna call?" He sounded frustrated, and his voice was growing louder. "Old Doc Jones quit making rounds through Cold Plains a year ago. And don't say you'll call one of those Devotee people to come out. Not on this ranch."

Susannah's whole body grew tense. "No, please. No doctors."

Maria came over and bent to smooth a hand over her hair. "There's a new man, sugar. Just came to town a while back. Don't know it for a fact, but local people claim he doesn't belong to the group. He's supposed to be a good doctor without ties to them. Or at least he don't spout that crud like the rest. I think we need to try. For Melody's sake."

She wasn't thrilled to hear Maria bad-mouthing the

Devotees' philosophy. What was so wrong with becoming a great new person? But the idea that her daughter needed medical attention was the central most important thing to her right now.

Looking to Nathan, Susannah pleaded, "Please help my baby. I know you won't let any of the Devotees take her from me. But Melody needs a doctor. We have to call this new man now."

"I'll call. But afterward, you remember what I said."

"Of course. We'll leave as soon as Melody can travel."

"The child shouldn't travel for at least ten days."

"What?" Nathan barked at the doctor. "Why not?"

Before he'd called the man, Nathan had dialed up May Frommer for a recommendation on the doc and also for a brief discussion of his current uninvited guests. May had said it was still up in the air as to whether Dr. Rafe Black was secretly a Devotee or not, but her best guess was he was not. And then she went on and on about how Nathan should be gentle with Susannah and the child—as if he was ever too rough on any woman. He simply wanted her gone.

"The baby seems lethargic because she's dehydrated," Dr. Black answered and brought him back to the moment. "I've given her electrolytes, but this kind of thing takes a toll on infants. Babies take cues from their mothers. In this case, the mother is anxious and exhausted, so the baby is, too. Stress can kill a child that small."

Hell, he was no ogre. He couldn't throw them out now.

"Have you treated the mother yet?" He wondered what Susannah would have to say about the doctor's orders. "Have you talked to her?"

"Not yet." The doctor picked up the second case he'd brought into the house and looked ready to go back into the bedroom.

But he turned first and asked a question of his own. "Is this woman a Devotee? She looks familiar, like I've seen her in town. But Devotees don't often come to me."

"She was a Devotee for a few months. Having the baby seems to have changed all that." Nathan hoped to hell that what he just claimed would turn out to be the truth.

He had no intention of having a practicing Devotee on his ranch, in his house, in his damned bed.

"But she lived in Cold Plains during the past six months?"

It was an odd way of putting the question, but Nathan nodded his head.

"Very well. I'll go back to treat her now. Your housekeeper tells me her name is Susannah and that she has a few cuts that qualify for suturing. I'll check them out."

Nathan let him go and then headed off to find Maria.

He didn't have to search long. He found her where she was most of the time: in the kitchen.

"Looks like you're going to have houseguests for the next couple of weeks," he told her. "Hope you're ready."

"The doctor says they have to stay? Good. We'll handle it. I'll fix you up a spot in one of the guest rooms."

Damn. "Why can't *they* move to a guest room?"

"Rooms are too small and there isn't one that's connected to a bath. This won't be forever. Don't whine about it."

Gritting his teeth, Nathan got his temper back under control. "What did you think of Rafe Black? The way he talked to me about the Devotees, I got the distinct impression that he wasn't one of them."

"Naw. He's no Devotee. He don't stink like they do."

That made Nathan chuckle. All right, so he was stuck with Susannah and the kid for a couple of weeks. He'd make the best of it. For quite a while now, he'd been wondering if it was possible to deprogram a Devotee. Actually, he guessed what he would be doing in this case was called exit counseling since Susannah left of her own free will. Once, before circumstances made him give up the idea, he'd been sure he could accomplish the steps necessary.

This might be a good time to find out for sure.

"There's only one wound I see that might need a couple of sutures. But it's probably been too long to keep it from scarring." The doctor spoke softly to Susannah even though Maria had taken the baby into the kitchen.

"Which wound? Where is it?"

"On the back of your arm. It won't show unless you wear sleeveless blouses or bathing suits." He opened his bag and took out the necessary equipment. "I'll make a couple of quick sutures to be sure it heals without any trouble."

"Thank you." She bit the inside of her cheek and waited for him to numb the area.

While he worked, Dr. Black said, "Haven't I seen you around Cold Plains? Have you lived there long?"

Was he asking her because he was a Devotee or because he wanted a new patient?

"I lived there for a while. But I'm leaving town tonight. Why?" She held her breath, waiting for his answer.

"Afraid you can't leave the ranch just yet. As I told Mr. Pierce, the baby needs at least ten days' rest and regular feedings before you two can travel."

"You told him that? What did he have to say?"

The doctor's eyebrows went up. "He didn't seem pleased, but he agreed."

Well, that was a relief. However, if the two of them were staying on the ranch, she would have to find some way of getting around Nathan. They couldn't conduct World War III between them for the next couple of weeks. It wouldn't be good for Melody.

"I'll give you instructions before I leave." Dr. Black finished working on her, and whatever he'd done hardly hurt at all.

But as he put his things away, he seemed to have more to add. Was there something very wrong with the baby that he hadn't told her?

"Could I ask a favor?" he asked softly.

"I guess so. What is it?" This was an odd way for a doctor to start a conversation, but she waited to hear the favor.

"While you were living in Cold Plains, did you happen to meet a woman named Abby Michaels? She was a new teacher's aide at the day care center. She disappeared from town a while back, and I'm trying to find out if she had a baby with her."

"The name kind of rings a bell." Susannah had been told by the Devotees that she was to become the new teacher's aide at the day care center after Melody's birth. Guess they would need to find someone else now. "But sorry. I didn't know her. And I never heard anything about a baby."

A sad look crossed the doctor's face for a second.

"Well, thanks anyway for trying. You can put on your shirt while I jot out a couple of prescriptions."

Out of the blue it occurred to her that this man was definitely not one of the Devotees. But wasn't it strange that any doctor would come to Cold Plains without intending to join the group?

Still… "Um, can I ask a favor now?"

"Yes." He looked over warily.

"I don't want the Devotees to know I'm here. I would prefer that they think the baby and I have already left town. Is there any other way besides writing prescriptions with our names on them?"

He gave her another wary look, and then his features relaxed. "I have samples of the necessary medications in my office in town. If the ranch can send someone for them, I'd be happy to offer what you need."

Breathing a sigh of relief, she nodded. Then she filed the info about him being so helpful away in her mind—just in case Melody might need more of his help.

"Would you like to go for a walk?" Nathan had waited until the baby was napping and Maria had time to sit with the little girl. "It's been a couple of days since you came to the ranch, and I thought you'd like to look around. Maria can keep an eye on Melody for a while."

Since the doctor had issued his orders yesterday afternoon and finished up with his patients, Nathan hadn't seen much of Susannah. She'd slept for almost twenty-four hours straight, and Maria delivered her meals on a tray.

But Nathan had stayed busy, studying his books and manuals on how to best manage exit counseling for ex-cult members. He just wished she had other family members whom she already trusted. The process of exit counseling depended entirely on establishing a reasonable and respectful level of communication with the ex-cult member.

The two of them had hardly gotten off to a reasonable and respectful start. But he would try. He thought she was worth the effort, and the baby deserved a whole mother who could think clearly.

"I'd enjoy a little walk. I've always wondered what a working ranch would be like."

"Get your coat." He waited at the bedroom door as she pulled on her tattered jacket.

He stared at the patched coat. Obviously, she needed a few decent things to wear. But she'd been ordered not to leave the ranch to go shopping. Nathan supposed they could order clothes off the internet, but that would still leave a few days for shipping. He came to the conclusion his original idea for gaining her trust might prove to be the perfect trick for solving both problems.

"Most of the work on the ranch happens well before dawn," he told her as they moved through the house toward the kitchen door. "Not too much going on late in the afternoon. But you'll probably get a glimpse of the stock as they settle for the night."

She nodded as he opened the door and escorted her out into the sunshine.

"There's also a couple of important people you haven't had a chance to meet yet, and I thought now might be a good time."

"Oh? Who are they?"

He slid her arm through his as they strolled out into the yard. "That's a long story. Mind if I talk while we walk?"

"Not at all. But we'll have to take it slow, I'm afraid. I didn't realize how weak I'd be."

Turning to her, he tried to keep his voice calm and reassuring. "Are you sure you feel well enough to walk?"

Her facial expression suddenly drew down in a frown. "I'm sorry. I didn't mean to ruin your walk. I can try harder. Or you can take me back so you can go alone. I'm really sorry."

There, that was the first sure sign of cult programming. He'd just finished reading about the typical signs: anxiety, paranoia and constant fear of not pleasing the person in charge.

But why was this particular former cult member affecting him differently? Why was the idea of giving her counseling and trying to help her overcome her issues becoming so important to him? All he knew for sure was that seeing her weak and trembling, and knowing she had no one to trust, gave him an ache deep in his chest the likes of which he had never felt before.

Certainly he had a few trust issues of his own, but he felt positive he could get past them long enough to help her open up. He might not trust her completely, and he'd found himself fighting his base impulses where she was concerned. Impulses such as the way his heart thundered whenever her eyes welled up—or the way his gut clenched each time they touched. But his every instinct told him she would be worth all the effort.

He unwound their arms and then placed his arm around her shoulders to hold her upright. "You're the reason for the walk. When you get too tired, just let me know. All we'll do today is stroll to the fence to see the cattle and then back to the house for a short visit. Okay?"

"I'm sure I can make that. And I want to hear your story. What's it about?"

"Um…me, I guess. Or rather, about the ranch and my family."

"Oh, good. Go on."

"See, it was my granddaddy who first came to this land as a young man. He built the ranch from a few acres into the place it is now. But when his daughter, my mama, died young, he tried his best to give the rest of us a deep love of the land and the animals."

Susannah looked thoughtful, and he knew she was hearing between the words. Good. At least she was still capable of analyzing situations. Maybe her cult training hadn't had time to completely overpower her mind.

"Granddaddy's lesson took with me. I love everything about the land and the place and wouldn't want to ever live anywhere else. But I can't say as much for my siblings or my father."

"Is that who we're going to meet? The rest of your family?"

"Sort of. My father is still out of town on a buying trip, and my brother may or may not turn up for supper tonight. He has his own interests. And my little sister…"

Nathan tried to find a way to phrase this properly. "Well, Tara never did care much for the ranch. She was always a little wild. And she became lots worse after Mama died. When she was nineteen, she had a baby and didn't know who out of her many lovers should be named the father."

"Oh." Susannah's expression seemed to say she might be sympathizing with the woman she'd never meet.

"I don't think Tara tried all that hard to figure it out, frankly. She was happy letting Maria and her older brothers take charge of her baby's welfare."

"Lucky she had family to count on."

Interesting comment. Didn't she ever have family to count on?

"Yeah, I'll say," he agreed. "You see, her little girl was diagnosed with autism when she was only two years old. Not three weeks went by after that before Tara hooked up with a new fellow. They left on the back of his motorcycle in the middle of the night. A few months later, we were notified she'd been killed in a motorcycle accident."

"Goodness. What happened to the baby?"

"That's who we'll be meeting. My niece, Sara. I'm her legal guardian. She's a wonderful little girl but needs a lot of help. I give her as much time as I can, and we've hired a woman who works with her and lives in her quarters."

A dark cloud crossed over Susannah's eyes, and she got a glassy look. "I'm not… I don't know if…"

Ah, hell. He hadn't given any consideration to the idea that meeting a child with special needs might make her worry about her own daughter's future. But he felt sure that was the fear he was seeing in her eyes.

What an idiot he was. He'd hoped to add to her trust by showing her how well loved and taken care of Sara was.

But how could he have hoped she would trust him about this when she obviously didn't trust him enough to tell him the whole truth about her background? Trust took time. He got that. But saving her was too important to give up.

"Trust me, Susannah. It'll be fine. You'll see."

"I want to trust you. Really, I do." Her face was a mask of indecision. Then she said, "I'm glad you told me about your sister. I have something to tell you, too. I wasn't completely honest when I said my ex-boyfriend, Melody's biological father, was a traveling salesman."

He felt his jaw tighten but he couldn't help it.

"Uh, well, he *did* travel." Susannah's eyes grew large as she watched his reactions carefully. "And he was selling stuff. But the stuff he sold was drugs. He told me he was a wholesale dealer."

Nathan took half a step back. He should've known there was more to her story. He'd been right not to trust her completely.

"I'm sorry I didn't tell you the whole story before," she added quickly. "I just didn't think we'd be staying on the ranch long enough for it to matter. And I never got involved in his business. Really. I never saw him take the drugs, either. He could've been selling anything for all the difference it made in our lives."

It was easy to see how sorry she was about lying. And the longer he stayed silent, the more her eyes welled up again. Ah, hell.

"It's okay," he finally managed, and was surprised to find he meant it. "I believe you weren't involved in his business. And that maybe your relationship had just been a bad choice. Let's put it behind us and go on from here. I still want to help you, and I still want you to meet my niece. Okay?"

She nodded and blinked her eyes a couple of times. She looked so vulnerable and afraid that his gut turned over again. Apparently, she still hadn't told him the whole truth. But whatever this new little untruth was would have to wait.

Jeez. Why he was so determined to help her was still a mystery. But, by heaven, he vowed she would be free of her cult programming before she and her child had to leave the ranch for good.

Maybe helping her would make a good start to easing his guilt over the death of his ex-wife. And a start, but by no means the end, of what he intended to do in the memory of all the women who'd been taken in by that slippery con man Samuel Grayson.

Chapter 4

Trembling, Susannah followed Nathan down a winding path ringed with rosebushes. Had she done the right thing by telling Nathan about Melody's father? She'd almost confessed the whole ugly truth of her past. But the look on his face when she'd told him about the drugs made her hold back.

Luckily, he'd seemed to overcome his shock about her confession fairly quickly. The rest of the past would have to stay buried. It wasn't that she thought he would force her to leave if she told him. She trusted him not to rub it in her face. Somehow she knew he wasn't that kind of man.

Still, what good would it do to blurt out everything? She and Melody would not be staying on the ranch for good. It was impossible. So why take the chance of upsetting him for no reason?

He was a beautiful, honorable man. She had lots of

feelings about him. Some just as honorable, some not so much. And she had no intention of ruining whatever temporary relationship they could have by shoving unnecessarily hurtful truths about her past in his face.

They were making their way to what appeared to be a new wing. Low slung and cozy, the construction made it look more like a cottage rather than part of the ranch house itself.

She set her shoulders, not at all sure she was ready to meet a special-needs child. But then, she didn't know what to expect. All she knew was that the Devotees would not be happy knowing such a girl lived in close proximity to their perfect world.

The more she'd been thinking about the Devotees' stance against any imperfections, the more uneasy she'd become. How dare the Devotees shun people who weren't like them? Surely Samuel couldn't know about this way of thinking.

And what about the rumor of their selling imperfect babies? To whom? And for what? The very idea gave her the chills.

"Here we are." Nathan stood on the stoop with one hand on the doorknob. "Kathryn wants to meet you, too. She's offered a few things for you to wear if the two of you are the same size. You're not too tired?"

Before coming here they'd only gone a little ways past the yard and around the barns out to the nearest wooden fence. From there, in the distance she'd seen a field full of reddish-colored cattle, milling about in tall grasses and making soft noises. It'd been interesting, especially when Nathan told her how much work it took to raise a herd in Wyoming winters.

But now he was waiting for an answer to his question. "I'm okay." She wanted to do this to please him.

In the sunshine, for the first time since she'd come to the ranch, she was able to breathe deep. With Nathan standing beside her, she'd felt really safe for the first time in weeks.

As he'd talked about the cattle, she'd casually glanced over at him. The sun had hit him just right, and glints of gold bounced along his body like spotlights. The sudden rush of sensual awareness caught her by surprise.

She had no business checking him out like that. Closing her mouth, she tried to concentrate on what he was saying.

But heaven knew he had a body that could make any woman weep. Tall and lanky, his arm muscles bunched under the long-sleeved shirt. Here was a man who worked hard outdoors and came by his muscles naturally. She'd never met anyone quite that rugged before. Her fingertips longed to run along the plains of his well-honed body.

Still, she fought the unwanted urges and chided herself for even thinking such things about a man who temporarily had control of both her and her child's well-being. And in addition to that one very important fact, she was also a brand-new mother with an infant and not a woman on the prowl for a man.

Nathan's only reason for being nice to her had to be Melody. She felt sure of it. He'd taken them in and agreed they could stay because he was a decent person who couldn't turn away a sick newborn. Susannah had done nothing but give him trouble thus far.

So, if he wanted her to meet his niece, then she would do it despite her reservations.

He pulled off his Stetson and led her inside the house to a small living room, like something out of an ancient TV sitcom set back in the fifties. "Kathryn? We're here." He ran the rim of the Stetson through his fingers and waited for acknowledgment.

"Come on back." A pleasant female voice came from somewhere unseen. "We're just finishing afternoon floor time."

Nathan motioned for her to go ahead through a set of double doors. On the other side, she found another great old-school-style room with little girls' toys spread all over the floor. And in the middle of the mess sat a pretty little girl of six or seven with long blond hair.

The girl didn't turn when they came through the door. In fact, she didn't acknowledge their presence at all.

Not so was the case of the woman with her. The nice-looking woman of about forty was getting to her feet, smiling at Nathan as they came closer.

"Glad you could stop by this afternoon before she gets too tired. Sara's made a couple of emotional connections today, and I'm sure she'll be happy to see you." Then the woman turned to Susannah and stuck a hand out. "Hi. You must be Susannah. I'm Kathryn Robards, and this is Sara Pierce."

"Good to meet you." Susannah took Kathryn's hand but noticed the little girl did not even turn at the mention of her name.

Was this child mad that a stranger had come to visit?

Nathan dropped his hat on a nearby table. Then he folded all of his six-two or six-three body up and sat on the floor directly in front of the child.

"Hi, Sara. What are you playing with today?" He picked up a nearby doll and brought it up to his face. "This little princess? She's one of your favorites, isn't she? Want to play?"

Sara looked up at Nathan, and her eyes widened. She reached for the doll, still not smiling, but more animated than she'd been since they'd come into the room.

"Uncle Nat-ton. Jasmine, p...please."

Nathan chuckled and handed her the doll. For a few minutes, he spoke softly to her about the toy. His voice stayed low and slow. But his face spoke volumes about how well he loved this child.

"Do you know much about autism, Susannah?" Kathryn spoke in a quiet tone while Nathan and Sara continued talking and playing on the floor.

"Nothing. She doesn't look physically injured or ill in any way."

"No, many autistic kids seem like perfect children on the outside, though unfortunately Sara is one who has gone through her share of physical challenges. But we've got most of those managed now. You might not know, but it's a fact that some autistic children have high functioning intelligence. We think Sara may well be one of them. However, everything is all locked up inside her head. Nathan hired me a couple years ago as her companion and to work with her on ways to expand her abilities."

"Does she go to school?"

"No, not yet. But we're hopeful that someday she will. Would you like to talk to her?"

"Very much."

"Then you need to know that she will appear disconnected, but she's not. Autism robs these kids of the ability to use regular facial expressions. At first glance, the rest of us can't tell if she's happy or sad. That might make you think she isn't clever, but she's far from dull or mentally impaired.

"The rest of us just need to express things in a slow

and steady way with her." Kathryn gave Susannah a friendly and encouraging smile. "If you show you're interested, she will be, too. You'll do fine. Give her a chance. She managed to dress herself this morning. That's a big breakthrough."

Unsure of what she would do or say, Susannah nodded and went to sit on the floor next to Nathan. He introduced her again to the child with still no visible sign of acknowledgment from the girl. Susannah didn't know what to expect. But in the next moment, Sara grabbed a baby doll off the floor and turned to her. Without looking directly in her eyes, the little girl offered the doll.

"Baby."

Susannah was surprised that Sara had spoken, but she took the doll from her hand and looked it over. "Pretty baby. Does she have a name?"

"Baby."

"Well, Baby's a nice name. I have a baby, too. A real baby. But her name is Melody. Would you like to meet her sometime?"

Nathan interrupted. "I'm not sure Sara knows what a real baby means."

"Real." The little girl actually looked up into Susannah's eyes. She could swear the child was smiling even though her lips never moved from their stationary position.

"Oh, yes." Susannah rocked the doll in her arms. "Melody cries and eats and wets her diapers. She's real."

Sara turned to her uncle, and Susannah could swear she wanted to ask him something, but no words followed.

"I think Sara might like to meet Melody." Nathan's

voice sounded raspy, full of sudden emotion. "We'll see how the baby is faring tomorrow. In the meantime, it's time for both Sara and Melody to eat supper, don't you think?"

With silent encouragement from him, Susannah turned the doll around and gave it back to the little girl.

Kathryn came over and touched Sara on the shoulder. "Time to clean up, sweetheart." She bent and began picking up the dolls and toys. "Maria is probably almost ready in the kitchen. Are you hungry?"

Sara dropped the doll and got to her feet. Suddenly disconnected from the rest of the world around her, she walked out of the room. Kathryn went after the girl, bidding her and Nathan goodbye over a shoulder.

Nathan spoke first. "Amazing. I've never seen Sara take to anyone so quickly. She actually looked at you almost right away."

Susannah's heart thumped and broke a little for the motherless darling. "Will she get any better? Poor child. Will she ever be able to go to school? Ever smile?"

Nathan stood and held out his hand to help her up. "I hope so. We're doing everything we know how to do to see that she does."

She let him pull her to a standing position. "Is it really okay if I come back tomorrow to see her?"

"If you like." Nathan sighed. "It should be good for her. And maybe seeing the baby will help her, too. Bring Melody here as soon as you think it's possible."

"Thank you. I should probably get back to Melody now."

"You're welcome, Susannah." He took her by the hand. "We'll cut through the garden to the main house."

Susannah felt a tingle at his touch. She'd liked the feeling it gave her when Nathan had smiled at her.

Maybe she'd liked it a little too much. He was just being polite. She slid her hand out of his and stuffed it in her pocket.

"You know," he began, "when you're feeling up to it, feel free to scout around the house while Melody's napping. We have a wonderful library and an office with a couple of computers you might find useful. Make yourself at home inside the house.

"But if I were you, I'd be careful outside," he added thoughtfully. "Lots of ways of getting hurt on a ranch. And you never know when those Devotees might decide to show up again. Just ask a hand or Maria to go along if you want to look around outside. I'll be available as often as possible. Okay?"

Better than okay. "That's very nice of you. I hate to put you to all the trouble."

"No trouble. You might as well find productive ways of spending your time while you're stuck here."

All of a sudden Susannah had a vision of one way she'd sure like to be spending her time—with those strong arms wrapped around her while she kissed him senseless.

But that was beyond crazy. She'd be lucky if the two of them could manage to build a friendship in the time she was here. Romantically, she was so far out of his league that she should stop even considering such a thing.

Still, she had a feeling that no matter what she told herself, he would be starring in all her daydreams from now on.

Tired and sweaty after spending the day on the range with the hands, Nathan stomped into the mudroom of the house, debating whether or not to stop in the kitchen for a beer before he hit the shower. He hadn't seen Sara since early this morning and hadn't run into Susannah at all.

A beer wouldn't help him with either female, he decided with regret.

"Nathan," Maria called out to him from the kitchen.

Taking off his boots, he let her know he'd be right there. He sure hoped he wouldn't have to deal with any household problems tonight. He had plenty on his plate already.

When he walked into the kitchen, he spotted his father sitting at the table, talking with Susannah. Great, just what he needed. His father hadn't had a civil word to say to him in five years.

Maria handed him a cold, long-necked beer without asking. "Your father is back in town."

"So I see." He took a swig from the bottle despite his earlier decision against it. "How'd the auction go?"

"About like you'd expect." His father sounded as grouchy as ever. But then he looked toward Susannah and smiled. He *actually* smiled.

"You've met one of our new guests, Dad?"

"Yes, Susannah and I were having a nice chat. I'm looking forward to meeting her baby when she's awake."

Susannah beamed. "I'm afraid that doesn't happen too often. Melody needs a lot of sleep."

His father reached over the table and patted Susannah's hand. "Maybe I'll sneak a peek while she's sleeping, then. Babies are worth waiting for."

Nathan took another swig of beer…and then another.

Maria cleared her throat. "Go on and clean up, Nathan. We'll be eating early tonight. Kathryn tells me

Sara is eager to join the rest of us for dinner, so the whole family will be at the table at the same time."

"Even Derek?" Nathan was stunned. He could count on one hand how many times in the past year he hadn't eaten alone. Did his brother even still reside on the ranch?

"Yes." Susannah was the one who answered his question. "I met your brother earlier and convinced him to join us for dinner. He said he would set up a baby monitor so I could hear Melody here in the kitchen. I'm also afraid I may've been the one who suggested dinner with Sara. But Kathryn says she's ready."

Irritated at his impossible father and ghost of a brother, Nathan stared at Susannah as a myriad of things swirled through his mind. She'd certainly had a busy day for herself. He would like to talk to her about her opinions of Sara. And he would love to know how the hell she had gotten close to everyone in his family but him in such a short time.

Laurel, his deceased ex-wife, hadn't been at all close to his father and brother, and she'd known them for years before she died. Was it because Susannah was sweeter and had a much brighter smile? The last few years of her life, Laurel had been unhappy most of the time. Or maybe it was because Susannah seemed so vulnerable. Any man, even his cold, distant father and his lazy, hermitlike brother would want to get close to Susannah in order to protect her. She sure brought those feelings out in him.

He stayed silent while finishing the rest of the beer, trying to figure her out. He'd planned on giving her a day or two to settle in before he tried the exit counseling techniques he'd reviewed over the past few days.

But it looked like she was a lot quicker at settling in than he'd imagined.

Giving up on coming to any immediate conclusions about her, except for the fact that she was one of the most beautiful women he'd ever met and she didn't seem to recognize that fact, he placed the bottle on the counter and took off toward the bathroom to clean up.

"Supper's in fifteen minutes," Maria called after him.

"I'll be there." He was confused, annoyed and lusting after an unattainable woman, but he'd be there.

After supper, Susannah came back to the kitchen after feeding Melody to find that everyone had finished and had already gone—save for Maria. The older woman stood working at the sink on a mountain of pots and pans.

"Can I help with the dishes?" She turned the baby monitor on but didn't expect Melody to stir for a while yet.

"That's all right, sugar." Maria was one of the sweetest-natured people Susannah had ever met. "Nathan's gone to tuck in Sara, but he said he'd be back to help dry."

"I can dry."

Maria shot her a grateful look. "Well, I don't suppose it would hurt to get a head start on things. Thanks. Grab one of those dish towels and then stack the ones you finish over on the sideboard."

"I like helping. It makes me feel useful and not so much like a leech." Now, why had she said that? Those words were echoes of a long-ago time that she'd sworn to forget.

Maria didn't appear to notice. She went right on washing.

"You sure made good impressions on Mr. Pierce and Derek." Maria handed her a deep pot. "I don't believe I've seen Mr. Pierce smile that much since before his wife died."

"He's a nice man." Susannah had liked him right away. "Easy to talk to. I just wish Nathan was that easygoing. He sure seemed angry at me tonight, and I don't know what I did."

"Now, honey, he didn't look angry to me. Just his usual tense self around his father. That's all. But that has nothing to do with you."

Susannah finished drying the pot and started on another. "They don't get along? That seems odd. They're so much alike."

"They used to get along real well. But a crack opened up between them after Nathan's grandfather died."

She would've thought that might've brought them closer. "Do you mind if I ask what happened?"

"It's no secret." Maria stacked another wet pan on the counter. "Nathan's father took over as the head of the ranch when Derek didn't want nothing to do with the day-to-day work of it. See, Derek inherited, but he's not interested."

"So Nathan thought he should have been the one to take charge? I sort of got the impression that Nathan does most of the work."

"Yes, he does. But I don't think Nathan would've cared much about his father grabbing the power if it hadn't been for something Mr. Pierce did right afterward."

This was getting too personal, and Susannah was

almost afraid to ask, but her curiosity got the better of her.

"Um…what did he do?"

Maria stopped washing for a moment and turned to her. "He sold off the property around that old creek. The land wasn't bringing in anything to the ranch. Too many trees and too rough for grazing. But Nathan dearly loved that piece of land. Used to fish the creek with his granddad."

"The creek?" Suddenly it hit her. "You mean the one that runs behind the Cold Plains Community Center? The one that has healing powers? But that belongs to Samuel and the Devotees. It's…"

A deep voice broke into her sentence. "There's nothing special about that creek water." Nathan appeared beside Maria. "Nothing except it still should belong to the Pierce ranch like it always has."

"Nathan." Susannah felt a rush at seeing him and nearly dropped the pan she held.

"The water in that creek has no special properties." He nearly shouted at her. "It's water, plain and simple. I don't care what Samuel Grayson tells the suckers who pay good money for it."

Oh, no. He was angry again. She felt lots more comfortable in his house when he wasn't mad.

Whatever she was doing to set him off, she just had to find a way to smooth things over with him for good.

Chapter 5

Nathan jerked a dish towel off the counter and took one of the pans from Maria's hands. He shouldn't let talk of Samuel Grayson and the Devotees bother him this much—especially since he was determined to give Susannah exit counseling and needed to remain non-judgmental, calm and loving. At least, that was according to the textbooks.

"I'm sorry if I said something wrong, Nathan." Susannah looked at him through terrified eyes, as though he might strike her at any moment.

Dang it. Some counselor he was turning out to be. Not only did he need her to look at him with respect and without all this terror, but someday he wanted to see her looking at him with a little of the same sexual tension he knew they both felt. At the moment he was acting more like a tyrant than a lover.

He took a breath and then forced a smile. "I'm not

angry at you. It's just the mention of Samuel Grayson that riles me. If you knew what I know about him, I think you might agree with my position."

Her eyes went glassy, and she stood frozen for a moment too long.

Finally, Maria interjected a cheerful break in the tension. "Susannah, you might want to listen to what Nathan has to say. I'm sure if you do you'll see a different side to some of the things going on around Cold Plains. It wouldn't hurt to listen, would it?"

"I suppose not." Susannah tried a half smile, but she didn't look at all convinced.

"How about if I spend the morning with you and Melody?" he offered, working hard to sound polite and even-tempered. "I'll take a few hours off so we can have a good talk."

"I can't ask you to ignore your work for me." Another extremely sober expression schooled her face as she stood rooted to the spot. "I know as it stands you aren't crazy about me being here. Please don't do anything you wouldn't ordinarily do on my account."

That sounded like more of her cult programming coming to the surface—too timid, too apologetic almost to the point of paranoia. Her exit counseling might turn out to be much more than he could handle.

Still, he had to try while he had a chance with her. The last time, he'd been too late. He refused to accept those consequences with Susannah.

"Let me worry about my time." He set down the pan he'd been drying and took her lightly by the shoulders in as friendly a manner as he could manage. "I would like to spend the morning with you and the baby. I want to."

Whoa. Electric tingles spiked up his hand and down

his spine from the spot where he touched her. Without warning, he'd wanted a lot more from her than just her trust. Sensual images of the two of them together nearly blinded him. Gritting his teeth, he tried to stem the sudden ringing in his ears and stood there like an idiot, pretending nothing was different.

Maria spoke up again. "If he wants the two of you to have a talk, I think you owe it to him to listen. Don't you?"

Susannah's eyes widened again, and her shoulders tightened beneath his grip, as if she was under assault by a Devotee. "Oh, yes. Of course. Certainly. What time would you like us to be ready?"

Sure she hadn't felt the same things he had, Nathan sighed deep and long, releasing her shoulders and hanging his head. "This won't be a death sentence, just a discussion. If anything I have to say upsets you too much, you'll be free to walk out."

Her shoulders relaxed, and he could see the tension begin to seep from her jawline. "All right. But I'd better go back and be ready for Melody's next feeding. I think I hear her starting to fuss again. Can we call it a night for now?"

"Sure." He felt like an ogre. "We'll take this up again in the morning after breakfast."

Susannah spun to the baby monitor on a far counter and shut it off. "See you tomorrow, then. Good night."

She disappeared out the kitchen door before he could say a word.

"You scare her." Maria began cleaning out the empty sink.

"You think?" Nathan ran a hand through his hair. "I don't know what to do about her. She's either looking at me as if I came riding in on a white horse and saved her and the baby from certain death, or she's shaking like a leaf in a Wyoming wind and staring at me as if I was the villain with a whip in my hands."

"Oh, I don't know. I'm seeing something altogether different in her eyes when she looks at you."

"What's that?" He knew what he'd hoped to see, but that didn't mean it was there.

Instead of answering, Maria began putting the dried pots away in the cabinet. "It might help if you didn't raise your voice. Just think of what she's been through. Heaven knows what them Devotees caused her to believe."

She fisted her hands on her hips and glared at him. "All those folks there in Cold Plains are in danger. You know that better than most. I swear, people don't leave the place alive. Susannah got lucky to find you, and I think she knows that."

Nathan knew all about the danger. He knew it well. He just hadn't been able to come up with any proof when he'd made his accusations to the FBI. It was like living next door to a fireworks factory. Any day the whole place could go up.

But this ranch belonged to his family. It was his heritage. And he was damned well determined not to be scared off his own land.

"I want to help her," he said softly.

"Because you never got the chance to help Laurel? Or because you're determined to get the better of Samuel Grayson?"

"Yes. And no." He was torn about his true motives. "It's more than that." Every time he looked at her, his body went hard and his brain turned to mush. "Susannah's got so much potential. I've never met anyone so patient, supportive and empathetic. She could be anything she wants to be. Don't you see that in her, too?"

"I do. And I can also see something more in your eyes when you look at her but believe she isn't paying attention."

Nathan wasn't about to get into this discussion. He knew what he'd felt on occasion bordered on pure lust, but he refused to drag it out for Maria to make fun of.

Even if he could make a dent in Susannah's cult programming, she and Melody would never be truly safe on the ranch. They couldn't stay forever or the Devotees would be sure to find them.

"It's getting late," he said, taking the chicken's way out. "I'd better go study up on those counseling texts again before morning."

He put the dish towel up to dry and turned to go. "Wish me luck with her."

"You don't need luck, son. Just follow your heart."

"Are you comfortable?" Nathan had made a big pot of coffee for her and had seated them both at the kitchen table.

"Uh, just a sec. Gotta turn on the baby monitor."

Susanna stood up and flipped it on. Jittery, she didn't know what to expect, but she was determined to avoid being bullied.

Sitting back down, she pulled her chair closer. "What exactly are we going to talk about?"

He tilted his head like it was no big deal. "Nothing much. You've already made the decision to leave the Devotees, which you must know I applaud. So this morning I'd like to find out how you feel about that. Can we talk it over?"

"Not much to say. I'd really started to love Cold

Plains, and I'm going to miss Samuel's lectures. But Melody and I had no choice."

"You've had some time to think over the decision and look back at what you know about the Devotees." His voice was steady, even, calm. "Have your attitudes changed any since you left?"

"About the Devotees? Definitely. Something is seriously wrong there. All the rumors can't be based on nothing."

"Hmm." Nathan sat back and took a sip from his mug. "I'm going to be honest with you. There's even more going on behind the scenes than you know. People, Devotees of Samuel Grayson, have died. Been murdered. And quite a few of us believe it was at Samuel's orders."

Closing her eyes as though that would shut out his words, Susannah shook her head. "How can you even suggest such a thing? He's a good man. All you have to do is listen to him and you'll know that. Maybe one of the Devotees…"

Letting her words die, she stared down into her coffee. "He changed my life, Nathan. He changed my whole worldview. He can't be a murderer."

"Okay, let's talk about how you're changed first and save the rest for another time."

Nathan cleared his throat and continued, "You feel changed. But now you have to go back to the real world. How are you going to manage without Samuel? I think what you've been through should be called *thought reform*. Samuel tells you how to think and the Devotees provide the insulated environment so their way is all you know. That's the definition of a cult, Susannah."

"No way." She didn't want to consider the possibility. But the more she thought about the Devotees and the rumors swirling about them, the more confused she became.

"Having trouble thinking clearly?"

"Maybe. My mind seems a little foggy. I never used to be like that."

"Well, recognizing that is a start in the right direction." Nathan stood and stretched. "Need to move around a little? Want a snack or something?"

She shook her head. "I don't…"

"Nathan?" A very deep male voice interrupted her sentence, followed by a knock on the open kitchen door.

"Come in, Mac. Something wrong?"

The man she knew as Nathan's foreman came into the kitchen. "Not that I know of. But Ford McCall is outside wanting to speak to you. He says he won't take but a few minutes of your time."

Nathan glanced at her, and the look in his eyes set her nerves on edge again.

"Who's Ford McCall?" She noticed her voice had developed a shaky tone. Shoving the chair away from the table, she stood on wobbly legs.

"A local cop. He works for the Cold Plains Police Department."

"A Devotee?"

"I don't think so. I've known Ford since high school, but I haven't had a chance to talk to him lately."

Nathan turned back to Mac. "Give it a few minutes. Go back to where you left Ford by the long route. Then show him in here to the kitchen. I'll talk to him."

Mac left the room, and Susannah felt frozen to the spot, unsure of what to do.

Nathan picked up her coffee mug, rinsed it and set it in the sink. "Go back to the bedroom with Melody. I'll call you when it's safe to come out."

She scurried out the door and didn't look back. What on earth would she do if the Devotees found Melody? She couldn't live without her baby. Losing Melody would kill her.

By the time she arrived back in the bedroom and quietly closed the door, Susannah was already hyperventilating. She knew it was crazy to worry. Nathan had promised that the Devotees would not take Melody. And for whatever reason, she trusted Nathan.

Regulating her breathing, she quietly paced the carpet and tried to clear her mind, but some of the things he'd said were reverberating in her brain. Instead of making her mind clearer, she felt foggier.

"Nate?" A sudden booming voice shot through her fog, so loud and clear she could swear it came from a few feet away.

"Morning, Ford. Long time." That was Nathan's voice. "Want a cup of coffee?"

She spun to the sound and discovered the voices were coming from the baby monitor. Had she accidently hit the wrong buttons when she'd turned it on in the kitchen?

"No, thanks," the other male voice replied. "I can only stay a few minutes. Mind answering a few questions?"

"That depends on the questions."

Susannah looked down and found she'd been wringing her hands. She stuck them in her pockets.

Someone cleared his throat. "I have a computer-generated photo of a woman I'd like you to look at."

"Who's in the photo, and why computer generated?" Nathan sounded hesitant. Was he afraid he would be seeing a photo of her?

"Give it a look. I had the police morgue shot photo-enhanced so that the bullet wound in the head would not distract from the rest of the identifying features."

Silence for a moment. Followed by Nathan's voice. "I don't recognize her. Should I?"

"I was hoping you would. Her body was found four years ago up the road in Greybull. So far, she's a Jane Doe."

"Why ask me? In fact, why are you doing the asking in Cold Plains?"

"Look, Nate. We've been friends a long time, right? I'm going to tell you a few things about this investigation, but I expect you to keep them under wraps."

"You have my word."

Nathan sounded so serious. She decided he must believe the policeman was not a Devotee or he wouldn't be willing to talk or even listen for this long.

She willed herself to also listen carefully through the monitor for the slightest problem. If necessary, she could take Melody out the window and hide.

"The FBI are involved," Ford said softly. "This Jane Doe's body had a tiny black *D* visible on her right hip when she was found. You know what that means, don't you?"

"I know." Nathan's sigh came through loud and clear. "My ex-wife's body had the same *D* tattooed on her right hip when she was found. It's Samuel Grayson's personal mark. The one he only puts on loyal Devotees."

Another moment of silence and then Nathan spoke again. "So, you think Samuel murdered the Jane Doe like he did Laurel?"

"Yeah. And like at least three other women we've found in the vicinity over the past few years."

Susannah swallowed hard and tried to keep the contents of her stomach from coming up in her throat.

"But, as in Laurel's case, no one can prove anything?" Nathan seemed to spit the words out.

"That's right. The only link between all the women is the *D*. I figured if I can pin down this woman's identity, I might be able to trace her movements back here."

Susannah could hear rustling but no voices for several moments.

Finally, Nathan spoke. "You said bullet wound to the head. Like my ex-wife's?"

"Similar. But we can't get a match on the bullets."

"We? The FBI? You can't be working with your police chief on this?"

"Bo Fargo? Not a chance. In fact, he'd fire my ass if he learned I was doing this investigation in my spare time."

Nathan's chuckle was low, but she caught it anyway. "I didn't think so. So who in the FBI? I hadn't heard they were anywhere around here. Except for Hawk. I did hear he and Carly may have gotten back together after all these years apart."

Now Ford seemed to be the one to hesitate. "Hawk is working on the problem—quietly. Our old high school buddy means to find answers this time around."

Both voices faded out of the monitor for a second. Then, Melody suddenly awoke from her nap. Instead of her usual tiny mewling sounds upon awakening, she let out the loudest cry her mother had ever heard coming from her baby's mouth.

Through the monitor, she also heard the policeman say, "Since when is there a baby on the ranch?"

* * *

Nathan didn't quite know what to do. He'd never heard Melody cry that way. Was the baby in trouble?

"Hold on a sec," he told Ford. "I'll be right back."

He raced down the hall to his bedroom and flung open the door only to find Susannah changing the baby's diaper.

"Has the policeman left?" Susannah finished and lifted the baby in her arms.

"No, not yet. Is the baby all right?"

"She's fine. I think she must be getting her strength back. And her lungs seem to be getting stronger."

He relaxed and willed his pulse to stop pounding. "I'll say. We could hear her clearly in the kitchen."

"What'll we do?" Her eyes had that vulnerable look in them again.

His gut twisted at the thought of her coming to any harm. "I think you two should meet my old friend Ford. I've come to the conclusion he isn't working with the Devotees."

To his surprise, Susannah nodded her head without any fuss. "I think you're right." Her lips turned up in the sweetest smile he'd ever seen. "We'll join you for a moment, but then I need to feed the baby."

Why was she suddenly so easygoing about meeting someone from the Cold Plains police?

The question must've shown on his face, because she laughed a little and said, "I heard your conversation. Somehow I must've hit the wrong buttons on the baby monitor in the kitchen and could hear every word."

She'd heard all that about his ex-wife's death? And about Samuel being a serial killer?

"Um, do you want to talk about what you heard?"

"Not right now. Maybe later. Let's go meet your friend." She turned and marched out the door.

Nathan tried to rationalize the turn of events. Maybe it was for the best. He'd been trying to find a way to ease her into accepting that Samuel was one of the bad guys. Maybe having Ford tell her first would pave the way.

She had to accept that Samuel was not all good and all powerful before she could shake her cult programming for good. He could hardly wait until Ford left to talk to her about it some more.

Speeding up his steps, Nathan hit the kitchen doorway shortly before Susannah and the baby did. "Ford, there's a couple of people I'd like you to meet."

Ford turned from the coffeepot just in time to see Susannah entering the room. His eyes went wide, and he set down the mug he'd been holding.

"Hi," Susannah said without even the hint of a smile. "I'm Susannah Paul, and this is my baby, Melody."

Ford nodded, but the questions were clearly swirling through his eyes. "I think I've seen you in Cold Plains, Ms. Paul. But you were still expecting the last time I saw you around town."

"Please call me Susannah, and Melody will be three weeks old tomorrow. I haven't been in town since then."

Nathan turned to Ford. "You're welcome to a cup of coffee if that's what you were about to do. I expect you'll want to hear Susannah's story."

"Thanks." But Ford never moved a muscle. "Susannah, aren't you a Devotee of Samuel Grayson's?"

It was her turn to nod. "If you'll give me a few minutes to feed Melody and put her back down, I'd be happy to tell you how things changed."

A thrill went up Nathan's spine as he heard her say

those words. She felt things had changed again? His positive influence might be working after all.

Instead of feeling overjoyed at the prospect of her being helped, however, his mind wandered off to all the things he would like to say—to do—to her when she was free of the cult's influence. Hell, this whole deal was getting more complicated by the moment.

Chapter 6

"So you're saying Cold Plains' pretty look is all a fantasy? That none of it is real?"

After two evenings of tireless talking, Nathan hoped to hell his exit counseling was finally getting through to Susannah. He'd had about enough.

"Yes," he answered wearily. "That's exactly what I've been saying. The beautiful people and the clean, neat buildings are a facade. They hide an evil underneath."

Part of the problem with working with her was working closely with her—too closely.

Frustration was leaving him weak, refusing to touch, longing to taste. Every muscle and nerve ending urged him to take her in his arms and kiss her until she understood what he'd been trying to tell her.

Making love with her would help them both. He felt sure of it. Close up, the look in her eyes telegraphed that she wanted him, too. But there were so many reasons why that shouldn't happen.

She was a new mother, and it was probably too soon. Besides, she'd been holding back something from him, too. He'd be willing to bet it was something deep in her past that affected how she related to a cult's claims. And as long as she was keeping secrets, he couldn't really trust her.

When he made love to someone, it wasn't just a casual fling. He'd never been able to swing that way like some of his friends—like his brother had in the past.

To him, becoming intimate was special, sacred.

She sighed, a resigned sound that almost warmed his heart and made him want to wrap her in his arms.

"I believe you. But it's still hard to accept Samuel as a murderer who rules the Devotees like you say." She looked up in his face with an expression of such longing that he forgot what the hell he was doing here. "Do you believe he really killed your wife? Really?"

They hadn't talked about what she'd heard—not once in the two days since she'd overheard his conversation with Ford.

It was time to tell her the whole story. "Would you like another cup of coffee?"

She shook her head. "I'm breast-feeding. I'm okay. Maybe a glass of water?"

He stood, mainly to think of where to start, and went to the cabinet. "Sure."

While he poured water into a glass and handed it to her, he began. "In the first place, at the time of her death, Laurel and I were divorced. When Samuel and the Devotees first came to town, she became enthralled with everything they had to offer. She started going to Samuel's seminars, and soon she was working out in their brand-new state-of-the-art gym and having lunch with other Devotees in one of their health-food cafés. It wasn't long before she wanted a divorce." He sat down beside Susannah so they could talk quietly.

"That must've been terrible for you. Did you love her very much?"

He'd been thinking a lot about that lately and didn't much like the answer he'd come up with. "Actually, we'd been drifting apart for a while. Laurel never really took to ranch life. I'd thought she and I should start a family right away, but she always held back. I think now that we were mismatched from the get-go. But back then, I convinced myself that it was all Samuel's doing, that he seduced her with pretty images, phony emotional support and smiling people to offer friendship."

"Yes, all those things are very tempting for someone who is already lost." Susannah tried a timid smile, but it lit up her entire face.

He was sinking in quicksand, wanting her so much he could barely breathe. Desperate to stay away, he forced his attention back to the story.

Clearing his throat, he went on. "When I realized what was going on over there, I decided to find a way to save Laurel. It didn't matter that we were already divorced by then. I felt responsible. I'd brought her to Cold Plains in the first place. And it was my father who sold Samuel the property that put him and the Devotees on their path to taking over the town."

Susannah bit her lip and reached out to take his hand.

The warmth of her touch sent electric currents directly to his groin, but he plowed ahead. "I studied as fast as I could. I took classes in psychology and spoke at length with a man who had debriefed cult members back in the eighties. I believed that I was nearly ready to try helping Laurel when she texted me one day out of the blue."

"Was she asking for a reconciliation?"

"No. She was asking for help. Her text said the Devotees were worse than I'd thought and to come quick."

"Did you? Did you go right away?"

Sliding his hand out from under hers, he fisted it and forced it to his side. "God, help me, no. It was late, and Sara was having a bad night. She was terribly little then, and I didn't dare leave her until morning when the housekeeper arrived. By the time I got to town at daybreak, Laurel had disappeared. She'd vanished. I rounded up a bunch of locals to go looking for her and eventually convinced the FBI that she hadn't left of her own free will. But no one could find a trace."

He drew in a deep breath, hesitating to finish. The story never got any easier. "They eventually found her body four weeks later in a ditch near Cheyenne. She was murdered, shot in the head, execution style."

"Did they ever find out who did it?"

Shaking his head, he closed his eyes and tried to keep a torrent of hatred for the Devotees and Samuel from spewing out of his mouth. "No," he finally managed. "Seemed she'd been dating that Jonathan Miller guy who was the personal trainer at Cold Plains Fitness. But he had an alibi and was cleared of any connection."

"I know Jonathan. Good-looking guy. He *runs* the fitness place now. Seems nice."

Nathan had to keep his hands balled to stop from shaking her. "Seems nice? Haven't you been listening to a word I've said over the past couple of days?"

Her eyes widened. "Yes, I have. I know now that just

because he seems nice doesn't mean he is. He's part of the fantasy."

"Miller was one of the guys who came looking for you the first day you arrived." Nathan really worked at keeping his tone neutral. "He's a scumbag. I'm sure he had something to do with Laurel's death, but no one's been able to prove it."

Susannah looked down at her hands in her lap. "I don't know if I'm smart enough or strong enough to beat the Devotees, Nathan. Not in the long run."

He tenderly laid a hand on her shoulder, trying to give her as much support as he could muster without taking her in his arms. "You left. Of your own free will. No one forced you. You're a lot smarter and stronger than you think you are."

"I don't know." She sighed again and then looked up. "What time is it?"

"Nearly nine."

"Oh. Kathryn's been sitting with Melody. Sara wanted to visit the baby this evening, and Kathryn and I made a deal. But Sara will already be in bed. I have to go."

"You and Kathryn made a deal?"

"Yes. She sits with Melody when I want to do something outside the house. I even express milk so Kathryn can feed her on occasion. In return, Melody and I sit with Sara when Kathryn has to be away from the ranch."

"That sounds like a good deal all around. Glad you and Sara are getting along so well."

"Me, too. She's such a doll. I just wish I could do something to help her."

"But you are helping her. By being her friend and playing with her, you are helping."

He meant every word of what he was saying. Fruitless wishing for more time to spend with his niece had become a way of life lately. It was a sad regret that nagged at the back of his mind all the time. Sara needed so much attention. He was happy that Susannah made the effort.

"I'd better go now." She started out the door but turned at the last minute. "Thank you for helping me, Nathan. And for taking me and Melody in. I wish I could think of how to help you in return. But I'll never be able to repay you for everything you've done. My outlook on life is changing, and it's all due to you. Thank you."

After she walked out, the tension finally left his shoulders. He hoped to hell she was telling the truth, that he had helped her to see things differently. But there was still that niggling feeling in his gut that until he knew all her secrets he would never truly be sure she'd changed.

People could say anything. And often what they said didn't match what they believed. He'd learned that lesson.

"You think you can handle the mare by yourself, little lady?" Mr. Pierce, Nathan's father, had just finished showing Susannah the ropes on how to curry a horse.

After never spending any time around horses in her entire life up to now, she'd suddenly discovered that she loved them. "Yes, sir. I know I can do a good job. You can count on me. Miss Lulu and I get along very well."

"Well, that's excellent. I believe you. I'll be right next door in the office going over invoices with Mac for a bit. You finish up the chores for us?"

"I'll do it, sir."

Mr. Pierce chuckled and shook his head. "You can call me by my given name. Evan isn't too difficult, is it?"

"No, sir. Uh...I mean, Evan."

This time he laughed out loud. "We've sorely needed a little sunshine and laughter around this place, Susannah. And your brand of smile sure makes the days go by in a hurry. Thank you."

He was thanking her? It was the first time in memory someone had taken the effort to thank her just for smiling.

Susannah turned to finish up with Miss Lulu after Evan left her alone in the stall. While she brushed and stroked the docile horse, her mind wandered to the other person in the household who she certainly wished would notice her smile.

Nathan. The man was infuriating. He'd more or less stopped working as her counselor a couple of nights ago. Now they barely saw each other in the evenings for dinner or ran into each other early in the mornings while she was on her way to take Melody to visit Kathryn and Sara.

And that was it. There were no more long hours lingering over the coffeepot. There were no more frank discussions. Their talks had petered out after he'd tried to probe into her past history—the time before she came to Cold Plains, before Melody, way back to when she was a child.

She never talked about that period of her life—not ever, not to anyone.

Nathan was different than most. He *could* be someone she might confide in at last. But she had a feeling he would be telling her soon that her time on the ranch was over. Melody was well. She was healthy and pink and staying awake for longer hours every day.

Why would Nathan want them to stick around after she and her child were well enough to leave? She'd already pushed the time limit Dr. Black had set. Ten days to two weeks, he'd said. But they were nearly to three. If she was bound to go soon, she couldn't turn over any more of her trust.

Oh, yes, her heart wanted to. But it would cost her too much when she had to leave.

She'd already fallen for the guy—crazy as that sounded.

Nathan obviously took extreme measures to keep the two of them from touching. So even though she occasionally saw lust in his eyes when he gazed at her, he must've decided he didn't want anyone as damaged as she was.

Leaning her forehead against the mare's flank, she tried to stem the tears…stupid tears. It was worthless and useless to cry over something you never had.

She sniffed the waterworks away and fought her blurry eyes by squeezing them shut. The horse moved a little under her forehead.

"Yes, Miss Lulu, you're done. You are such a good girl." Reaching over, she stroked the animal one last time. "See you tomorrow."

Time to go retrieve Melody and check with Kathryn and Sara. Though, Kathryn probably wouldn't mind if she stayed away for a while longer. Yesterday Kathryn said that Sara had made a ton of improvement since she and Melody had been visiting regularly.

Kathryn seemed to love the baby, too. Susannah never worried for one second about her child while she was with Kathryn and Sara.

Stepping out of the barn into the sunshine, Susannah stood still and breathed deeply. Yes, she loved it here. Too bad she was destined to leave soon.

"That's her! Grab her."

She turned to the sudden shouting only to find two strange men bearing down on her. Before she could comprehend the meaning of what was happening, the first man had her in his grip.

"Where's the baby?" The other man, a man she barely recognized as a Devotee, got right in her face and shouted.

That got through to her. Devotees! "Wait! You don't want us. The baby isn't perfect. Leave us alone!"

She struggled against the rough treatment, and the man who'd shouted slapped her in the face. "Shut up."

As the two strongmen began dragging her away from the barn and toward a waiting car, there didn't seem to be much chance of breaking free. Her only hope was making enough noise to garner notice.

Starting to scream, she braced for another blow, fully expecting more pain. It came, this time as the guy with his hands on her tightened his grip on her arms while the other man hit again. The blow only succeeded in making her scream louder.

"Cover her mouth, you idiot." The man who spoke took one of her arms and jerked it behind her back.

The other guy fought to cover her mouth with the palm of his hand. She twisted her head and tried to bite him.

"Hey!" Another voice sounded from somewhere nearby. "Stop! What the hell…?"

She couldn't see who was shouting, but she sure hoped it was someone who could help.

"Move!" The man who'd slapped her picked her up by grabbing her around the waist and started to run.

Tired and fighting a constant desire to ditch work and be with Susannah, Nathan was heading toward the equipment barn with his head down and frustration rampant in his veins. Done for the day, he wished he could disappear for the night rather than have to face that beautiful, vulnerable face across the supper table.

Lost in his thoughts of her, he jumped when he heard shouting. But those sounds were soon drowned out by a shotgun blast.

Whoa! What the hell was going on near the house?

Running as fast as he could toward the noise, visions of murder and destruction blinded him and made him stumble. Damn, damn, damn!

As he rounded the last corner of the barn, he saw a half-dozen men chasing after a sedan that was speeding away over low grasses, bumping along in the direction of the main road. Chaos and barnyard dust obscured his view.

It seemed to take too much time for his slow brain to clear. As the dust finally began to settle, he put two and two together. Those frigging Devotees must've had the nerve to show up on ranch property again. He hoped to hell someone had gotten a decent shot off and winged one. They obviously needed a lesson in manners. Don't come where you're not wanted.

But since the car was already almost out of sight, he slowed his steps until it hit him...Susannah. Had they gotten to her and carried her off?

His cell phone was out of his pocket before he could think of who to call. If he called the police looking for Ford, he might just end up with the chief, Bo Fargo, instead. And chances were better than fifty-fifty that Fargo was a Devotee and one of Samuel Grayson's top men.

Hell… Searching his mind for an alternative, Nathan came up with the FBI and Hawk Bledsoe. Sure that he still had the man's card in his desk in the ranch's office, he moved in the direction of the office and away from the ranch hands continuing to chase after the disappearing sedan.

But as he neared the office, he looked up and spotted something that lifted the oppressive ache in his chest— the same ache he hadn't noticed until this moment, the one that had sprung up to take him nearly to his knees from the moment he'd figured out that the intruders were Devotees on ranch property.

His father and Mac, half carrying and half holding up Susannah between them, were heading for the main house. Thank God.

Nathan hurried to catch up. "What happened?" he asked as he came closer.

His father explained over his shoulder. "I spotted them damned Devotees manhandling Susannah and called Mac out of the barn. He came running with his shotgun and fired a warning blast over their heads. He couldn't aim at 'em for fear of hitting Susannah."

Manhandling? "How badly is she hurt?"

"Not bad. It mostly scared her. But she'll be all right once we get her cleaned up."

Nathan stepped up next to Mac. "I'll take her from here. You call in the men and go back to whatever you were doing."

Mac nodded and turned away. Nathan put his arm around Susannah's waist and tried to hold her upright against his body. But when he noticed her wincing, he let loose.

"What hurts?"

"At the moment, everything." She looked over at him, and the sight of her bruised face made him wince, too.

He would kill the bastards who'd laid a hand on her. He'd do it with his bare hands. The idea of some sick screwup hurting her turned his stomach. It was everything he could do to guide her gently into the house.

"Dad, I'll see to her."

His father heeded his request and hesitated when they came to the kitchen door.

"You could do me a favor, though," he said to be polite. "Go on out to my desk and find Hawk Bledsoe's card. He wrote his cell number on the back. Call him. Tell him I want to see him."

"Should I tell him why?" His father was being a lot more agreeable and accommodating than he'd been in many years. The old man suddenly looked haggard and tired. His shoulders were stooped, and his face had turned a sickly gray.

"Just tell him to come. Tomorrow morning will be okay. He'll know why."

Nodding, his father spun around and headed off while Nathan led Susannah inside. His dad sure had changed since Susannah had arrived. Today the transformation would've been stunning if Nathan had had the chance to consider it.

The moment Susannah entered the warm kitchen and heard Maria humming in the background somewhere, she began to sob. Big sloppy tears flowed down her cheeks.

A new ache hit him square in the chest. "You're

okay. Everything's over now. Uh…" He was at a loss as to what to say.

"Nathan?" Maria's voice called out to him from the utility room. "Is that you already? Supper won't be for a while yet."

Susannah turned into his chest. "Don't let her see me this way. Please."

"It's not that bad," he told her without thinking. But then he realized it probably was as bad as she thought.

He'd been planning on having Maria clean her up and tend to the minor scrapes. "Come on back to the bathroom with me. I'll take care of you."

The tears came harder. "I…I can take care of myself."

"Nathan?" Maria, still unseen, was sounding worried.

"Yeah, it's me. Don't stop whatever you're doing. I'm going to clean up. I'll see you in a bit."

"Okay."

Susannah put her hand to her mouth and blinked her thanks. Then she put her head down and hustled off toward his old bedroom and bath.

By the time he made it to the bathroom behind her, she was already running water. The tears were stopped, but the streaks of dirt on her cheeks were heartbreaking to see.

"I can do this, Nathan. Really."

He shook his head but didn't bother to reply. "The first-aid kit is here in the linen closet. If you can splash water on your hands and face, I can clean up the worst of it with alcohol."

It took her a few minutes to carefully wash, and when she'd finished, she turned to him. "I guess I do need help. I'm afraid to look in the mirror. I appreciate the offer."

"Nothing I see is that bad. You have a bruise on one cheek that might turn purple later on. And you have a tiny scrape on your chin. But your face should be back to its normal gorgeous self in a day or two."

That actually brought out a smile but she didn't say anything.

"Have a seat where I can see you better in the light." He nodded his head toward the only seat in the bathroom.

She made sure the lid was down and sat. He bent to dab at her few scrapes with an antibiotic wipe.

One or two spots must've still been plenty raw, because when he went over them, she opened her mouth and breathed heavily. But she made not one sound of protest.

Dang it, this was one very special woman.

Without considering the consequences, he bent closer, concentrating his focus on her slightly open lips. They were too tempting, and his brain hadn't yet processed what his body was demanding.

He stopped a hair's breath away and waited for her to pull back. Instead, she sighed his name. The trust implicit in that sigh spurred him forward.

He'd imagined a gentle kiss to make her feel better and forget her pain. But he soon got lost in the touch of satin under his lips and fell into the passion of the moment. Deepening the kiss, his mind blanked as their tongues tangled and their breaths mingled.

She reached out and laid her hands on his chest, while at the same time making tiny moaning noises deep in her throat.

The sensual sounds, the sudden rush of adrenaline through his veins… It scared him to death.

He broke the kiss and backed up a step. "I…um… don't believe any of your cuts needs a bandage. The antibiotic ought to be enough to take care of it. There's also a bottle of aspirin in the kit. Take two. And a nice, hot bath should help."

She looked up at him with a bruised look in her eyes to match the bruise showing on her cheek. Damn it. He was such a jerk.

"I'll have someone bring you dinner in a while," he choked out past the lump in his throat. "And I'll go sit with Sara so Kathryn can bring the baby in here. Anything else you need, just call. Otherwise, I'll see you in the morning first thing. We need to talk."

He rushed out of the bathroom and out the bedroom door so fast that he almost missed her saying "Thank you."

Yeah, right. *Thank you, Nathan, for screwing with my head.*

What kind of moron would leave a vulnerable woman who needed him and had offered a momentary respite of pleasure? Could he be that far gone?

The whole idea of walking away from her that way sounded just as sick as those Devotee bastards with their kidnapping plans.

Nevertheless, he picked up the pace and disappeared.

Chapter 7

The baby was crying. Susannah rolled over, but her aching body kept her in bed. Oh, yeah, *that* had been only this afternoon. Being attacked by the Devotees was already becoming just a bad memory.

Using every bit of whatever willpower she had left, she forced her feet to the floor and pulled the baby into her arms. "Shush, darling. Mommy's here. Are you hungry?"

What a good baby. Susannah was thrilled her child wasn't one of those babies who cried all night and barely slept. At just over five weeks, she was waking up only once or twice a night.

Settling in against the pillows and adjusting the baby to her nipple, her mind began to wander back to a few hours ago when her breasts were aching for an entirely different reason.

Darn that Nathan. She'd wanted him to touch her

so badly. And he'd wanted her as much as she wanted him. His need would've been impossible to miss. And the kiss…whew, boy. It was hot.

So what happened? Where had she gone wrong?

Closing her eyes, she visualized the kiss again. From the moment his lips touched hers, she'd totally forgotten about her aches and pains. She'd been longing for him to kiss her since the day he had rescued her and Melody. But she'd never thought she would have the chance.

He was every bit as good a kisser as she'd imagined. She just knew that the two of them would fit together— at least physically if not emotionally or intellectually.

Not once in the whole time that she'd lived in Cold Plains had any man interested her sexually. And she hadn't been dead—only pregnant. She'd seen plenty of guys who were clean-cut, cordial and better looking than Nathan in a classic sense.

But as much as she had dreamed about making a home in Cold Plains for herself and her child, she'd never given one thought to spending that forever with any of the Devotee men—or any man for that matter until she'd arrived at the ranch.

Could she live here, raise her child and be happy with Nathan for good? Oh, heck, yeah.

She had yet to meet anyone on the ranch who wasn't nice to her and the baby. Everyone, right down to the ranch hands, treated her like she mattered.

Well, on second thought, she took that back. Nathan only sometimes treated her like she was a real person with wants and needs of her own. Their spectacular kiss came to mind again.

Other times, he treated her like he thought she was the biggest drag and one more chore he had to deal with. She wished he would stop walking away from her. She was dying to find out what making love to him would be like.

Okay, so Nathan didn't believe the two of them would ever make a couple. She got that. Maybe it had something to do with his ex-wife, Cold Plains and the Devotees. Or maybe it was because she would never be as bright and industrious as he was. She'd grown up knowing those hard facts about herself and had been told often enough to accept that they were true.

The baby fell asleep in her arms, bringing Susannah out of her little pity party. Wait a second. At least some part of Nathan wanted her. And she wanted him—for a night or two if that's all she could ask.

She came to a decision. There was no reason not to try. They might be terrific together, and she wanted to find out.

Turning to her sleeping child, she whispered, "At least once before we have to leave here. Your mommy needs to stand up for herself for the first time in her life. I owe it to you to become the kind of mommy you need."

"You're harboring this Devotee and her child on the ranch? Do you really think that's smart? I thought you of all people in Cold Plains would've had your fill of Devotees." Hawk Bledsoe stood with hands on hips and hat pulled low to shade his eyes from the morning sun.

Nathan wondered how best to answer. "It started off simple enough. She was lost and hurt. No threat at all." And now she was a threat? In one major way she was becoming a definite threat to his well-being.

"I planned on giving her a little cash and sending

them on their way. But the doctor said the child might die if I turned them out."

Frustrated, he looked out toward the herd grazing in the distance. "Now the whole danged place is enthralled with the two of them. I couldn't just shove her off the land, could I?"

Hawk stood quietly for a few seconds. "I see. She's *different* than the others. That it?"

Nathan turned back and caught the amusement in his old friend's eyes. "Well, she is, damn it. Besides, the baby has a birthmark covering half her face. Supposedly those Devotees would consider that a defect and take the child away if Susannah ever went back. I couldn't let anything like that happen to an innocent."

"Not you." Hawk scratched his chin. "So has she tried to convert you to the Devotee ways yet?"

"Just the opposite. I've been giving her the exit counseling I would've used on Laurel if I'd had the chance."

"Is it working?"

It was a good question, but Nathan wasn't about to say that to an FBI agent—even one who was an old friend.

"Might be."

Nodding, Hawk changed his position and straightened. "I've been meaning to stop around and talk to you about your ex-wife's death. I wasn't in on the original investigation."

"I remember."

"You mind running over it again for me?"

Nathan gave Hawk the basics, sliding past all the difficult emotions involved. The FBI agent listened patiently and asked a couple of pertinent questions.

Finally Nathan's curiosity got the better of him.

"Why are you delving into all this again? It's been three years since Laurel died."

"They found another body last month. That makes five we can connect to Samuel Grayson, but he's covered his tracks brilliantly so far. Nothing leads back to him directly except those damned *D*s. I thought I had a new lead, an informant of sorts, but that deal fell through."

"What are you going to do? Give up?"

Hawk's expression turned rock hard. "No chance. I'll keep at it. Someone else will turn up with new evidence. Someone like your runaway, but with inside knowledge, will decide they've had enough or be threatened one time too many by Samuel Grayson and be willing to talk."

Nathan didn't know what to say to that. But his fear for Susannah and Melody began crystallizing into something deeper.

"In the meantime," Hawk continued, "I have a small field team nearby, and we'll keep going over the body drops and rechecking evidence and witnesses. Something will turn up."

Hawk hesitated and pinned him with one of those lawman stares he had perfected. "What are you going to do, Nate, when the Devotees come back out here again looking for their runaway and her child?"

"Protect my property from trespassers. Wouldn't hurt my feelings at all if a couple of those bastards went one step too far and died for their trouble."

Hawk made a kind of coughing noise and shook his head. "Can't really recommend that course of action, old buddy. Though a few less Devotees to worry about wouldn't hurt my feelings, either. But armed conflict is not a good way to go. The chief of police in Cold Plains might just decide to arrest you for something like that."

"What would *you* do?"

"Well, that would depend on how much I cared about the woman in question. Exactly how much is that?"

"Hmm." Nathan didn't care to think about how he felt toward Susannah, let alone discuss it with Hawk.

"I see. Well, in that case, I'd pack her and the kid up and take a vacation out of town for a few weeks. Maybe stay gone for a couple of months while you think it over."

"I can't leave the ranch, Hawk. I have too many responsibilities."

"I've heard that story before."

"Yeah," Nathan said. "I remember a time when your Carly felt the same way about her daddy's dairy farm. Seems like that was what broke you two up a long time ago, wasn't it?"

There was silence and another of those strained glances.

Hawk didn't seem any more inclined to discuss Carly than Nathan had been about Susannah.

"My brother and my old man aren't worth much around the ranch," Nathan said by way of further explanation. "And my niece is special needs. I'm all she's got. I won't leave her."

"I hear you." Hawk resettled the hat on his head. "I've got another appointment. If you need any help here, give me a call. But think about what I said. If you can't leave, at least send the woman and child away to be safe."

"And where would that be?"

"Anyplace where there are no Devotees. They don't own the whole world, you know."

Nathan thanked his old friend for coming and saw him to his car. Then he turned his attention back to the stock and those downed fences in the eastern pasture. But while going about his business, he couldn't help searching his mind and heart for a solution to Susannah's problem.

Samuel Grayson and his gang were not going to win this one—not if he had one breath left to take a stand against the bastards.

"Good night." Susannah lifted a sleeping Melody higher against her shoulder and prepared to make her way back to the bedroom.

Kathryn and Nathan's brother, Derek, bid her goodnight and each went their own way, too. All of them had been visiting with Sara in her room for the evening, and it was past the little girl's bedtime.

As Susannah trudged across the garden, she thought about her day. It was one hell of a day. She'd so hoped this morning that Nathan would find a moment for her. He'd said last night that they needed to talk. But when she'd entered the kitchen for breakfast this morning, Maria told her he'd already left. He'd gone off to work in faraway pastures for the day.

Their kiss still haunted her. The feeling of his lips on hers continued to buzz through her veins. She wanted to talk to him about it but knew that was a lost cause. Nathan would never accept a nice long chat about intimate subjects. And besides, what she really wanted was to try another kiss. Ha! That didn't seem likely, either—not if he wouldn't come within shouting distance of her.

Still feeling bruised and achy from yesterday's attack, like someone had run her over with a truck, Susannah stayed in the main house nearly all day. In the morning, she'd spent more time than usual with Sara and Kathryn. And in the afternoon, Nathan's brother had shown her how to work his computer. She wished she'd had more time to learn from him. He was a great teacher, and someday she might need to get a job that required a minimum amount of computer knowledge. Up to now, she'd barely touched a computer except at the library for high school projects.

Her day had gone by quickly, but Nathan never returned to the house, not even for lunch or dinner. She missed him.

But deep down she'd secretly worried that what he'd wanted to talk about was her time being up on the ranch. Maybe it was for the best that she hadn't seen him all day—another twenty-four-hour reprieve.

On the way back to her room, she walked past the guest room Nathan had been using. It was right down the hall from hers. And every time she went past she hesitated, hoping he would be coming or going and that she would have a chance to see him.

This time she stopped and put her ear to the door. There was nothing, no sound. Sighing, she tried to convince herself that if he needed her he would make a point of finding her.

Fat chance. The only reason he would have for finding her would be to tell her to get out.

Turning on a deep sigh, she slipped into her room and eased Melody into her baby bed. As she gazed down at her wonderful child, she realized her little girl would soon outgrow the tiny crib.

Wasn't it time that she made new plans for the two of them? Somehow, she was sure the fantasy of living on the ranch and being in love with her rescuer would soon be over anyway. Maybe she should save some pride and try making a plan to leave on her own. But it was hard to do when all she could think of was Nathan.

An hour later, Melody had been fed and put back to sleep, and Susannah's hair was nearly dry from her shower. She lay in bed, staring at the ceiling in the low glow of the night-light, thinking about her situation.

She'd been so overwhelmed by finding a man like Nathan that she'd gotten caught up in the romance of it all. Yes, she did like it here on the ranch—a lot. But she didn't have the experience to make a career out of ranch work.

And yes, she'd fallen in love with little Sara, but she didn't have the knowledge or experience with special-needs children to make a career out of that, either. In fact, she wasn't trained for any career. The only honest jobs she'd ever held were babysitting and waitress work. Neither of those would provide enough for her to make a living and take care of her child.

Staying with the Devotees had sounded like heaven for an inexperienced single woman with a baby. They'd promised to take care of her every need, and all she had to do was believe what they told her and do the jobs they gave her.

From nearly the beginning, she'd had a gut feeling that things weren't as rosy in Cold Plains as the Devotees made them out to be. But, like her time on the ranch, she shoved aside her reservations and went with the flow.

Not anymore, though. Never again.

Nathan had changed all that. He'd awoken her to reality. He'd made her see things as they really were and stopped her from fantasizing.

Actually, she had to wonder how a person with her

background could've gotten herself into such a position in the first place. She should've been street-smart at least. Her childhood had not been exactly a dream. It was far from it.

Perhaps she'd subconsciously trained herself to blank out reality and live in a fantasy world full-time. That seemed rather likely from this new perspective of hers.

In fact, the whole disastrous affair with a deadly drug runner that had left her pregnant and destitute in Cold Plains had been just another kind of escape. She could see that now.

Nathan had given her the means to think more clearly. She loved him for that and for so many other reasons.

A single tear leaked from the side of her eye, but she ignored it. She was deeply and fully in love with a man for the first time in her life. But what did love mean? At no time in her background could she think of knowing a single couple who'd been truly in love.

People used each other, for comfort, for protection, for money, for stability, for power and for sex. But what was real love all about?

Digging deeper, and actually dredging up some of Samuel's seminars about family, it came to her. Being really in love meant you cared more about the other person's welfare than you did about yourself.

Did she? Is that the point she'd arrived at with Nathan?

An image of him standing in the sunlight with his clear blue eyes gleaming brightly and his light brown hair ruffled by the wind entered her mind. What would she give up for him?

Nearly everything, she supposed—everything but Melody.

Wasn't that an amazing fact? They hadn't even made love yet, and here she was truly in love. So what could she do to make him happy? Besides disappear? She'd already decided to take steps to that end.

What else?

Burrowing deeper into her sheets and relaxing, she tried to think about what would please Nathan the most. What did he want?

An image of Samuel came to mind, and she realized getting rid of the Devotees would go a long way toward pleasing Nathan. Yes, that would be a wonderful present. But she didn't have a clue how to go about doing that. The policeman who'd come to the ranch said he was investigating, but he knew how to do that sort of thing.

Darn that Samuel. He'd made a sorry mess out of so many lives.

A picture of his face, looking benevolently down at her with those vivid green eyes, reminded her of how stupid she'd been to believe his lies. Thank heaven for Nathan.

Another picture swirled in her head, dreamlike. Blue eyes, gazing at her with such intensity, she felt prickly all over. They were Nathan's eyes.

"I want you, Susannah." It was Nathan's voice, *rough and intense.*

"And I want you. Touch me. Please."

Warm lips gently pressed against hers, the heat from them traveling straight to her core. Next, his warm hands rubbed her achy breasts, stirring her beyond reason.

From out of the fog, someone moaned. Had that sound been her?

Suddenly a wet mouth went to her nipple, so tender,

so much pleasure. He sucked a hardened peak into his mouth, nipped at it, only to lick and soothe her once more. How had he known that was exactly what she'd needed?

Susannah wanted to touch him in return, but something was holding back her hands. She squirmed, ready to force herself out of the haze and take what she needed.

But she couldn't... "Please," *she begged.*

Rolling and kicking out, she blinked open her eyes to find herself in the low night-light of a darkened room. She discovered she was alone in the bed and tangled in the sheets. Panting and needier than she'd ever been, she turned to the clock and realized a half hour had gone by. She'd been asleep...dreaming.

Darn it. She'd been so sure that episode with Nathan had been real and that the sensual looks she'd sometimes see in Nathan's eyes had led him to do what he'd really wanted.

What Nathan really wanted.

She'd been trying to find a way to make him happy. Should she take the initiative and make them both happy?

Why not?

Sliding quietly out of bed, she tiptoed to the baby's crib and checked on her child. She was sleeping soundly. Judging by the past couple of nights, Melody should sleep for at least three more hours before she needed another feeding.

This might be the last night for Susannah to try convincing Nathan they would be great together. And the only thing to lose could be a little of her pride if he kicked her out of his bed.

She eased open the bedroom door, and leaving it

cracked so she could hear the baby, she crept across the hall to the guest room. Had he locked the door?

Trying it, she was pleased to find it open. The door swung inward without the hinges making a sound.

So far so good.

She held her breath and waited for her eyes to adjust to the darker room. Listening intently for any sound, she was thrilled to hear Nathan softly snoring.

Ten steps into the room and she was at the side of the queen-size bed. Did she really have the guts to go through with this?

It might be the worst idea she'd ever had—or it could be heaven. She would never know unless she tried.

It was now or never.

Chapter 8

Someone was in his room.

Groggy, Nathan forced his mind to focus. What the hell? His muscles went taut as he geared up to reach for his gun in the nightstand drawer.

The next thing he knew, the mattress shifted with the weight of someone climbing in beside him. Tensing, ready for a struggle to the death, he waited for the first blow.

But before anything else happened, he got a whiff of raspberry shampoo. Huh? He would recognize that scent anywhere. He'd smelled the same fragrance in every room of the house. He'd scented it on the wind in the pasture. It haunted his dreams.

Rolling to his side, he was astonished to find her reaching out for him. "Susannah."

"Please don't send me away. Not tonight. Just for to-night."

For all of ten seconds, he told himself that's exactly what he should do: send her back to her bed. Yeah, right…not a chance.

A sliver of moonlight crept into the room, giving him just enough light to make out her features in the shadows. The thin straps of her nightgown were visible against her pale skin. Swamping waves of longing washed over him as he gazed at her. He couldn't speak.

This was all wrong. Tomorrow he would begin the process of finding somewhere safe where he could send her to be out of the danger, out of his life.

But try explaining that to his body tonight. His mouth went dry. For endless moments, he gazed back at her. Her long, lush hair lay suggestively against her shoulders. Her limpid hazel eyes were deep pools of desire.

There must be some way he could stop things, some way to man up and do the right thing.

But nothing he did worked to put a stop to his burning desire. Next he tried telling himself she was a new mother and too tender to touch. That made sense. He wouldn't want to hurt her. But his rebellious fingers paid no attention, reaching over to stroke the contours of her face—he let them linger on her full lips.

Sensing the warm glow of her need under his fingertips, he outlined her mouth slowly. Not willing to let her go, he brushed her soft lower lip with his thumb.

She closed her eyes and breathed deeply. His eyes dropped to her breasts, heaving as if she'd just run a mile. He didn't need to see her naked to know the body under the thin material was lush and warm. Even in pitch darkness he would've remembered the smooth perfection of her skin and the generous curves so easy to spot under her clothes.

To hell with what happened tomorrow. He no longer cared about anything but the here and now.

Whipping away the covers, he flipped on his back and slipped out of his boxers. He needed to hold her in his arms, to feel something good and giving next to him instead of the excruciating loneliness of his bed since the divorce.

Turning, he held out his arms to her and she slid closer, making soft murmurs of contentment in her throat as she snuggled into his embrace. She fit as though the two of them had been doing this for years, as though she belonged beside him for good.

Easy, he thought when he caught her tender sighs and unquestioning trust with a passion-filled kiss. Easy does it, he reiterated as his hand closed over one breast.

Finding himself too clumsy for such a gentle touch, he bent his head and tasted her tip through the silken material of her gown. It was just a lick, only a taste and none of the things he would've liked to do to drive her wild.

Yet she seemed to go wild with any amount of pressure.

"I need you," she whispered.

She needed him? Holy hell. He was the one in deep need here. Everything about her sharpened his hunger to an excruciating ache.

Groaning, he held back, afraid to make a wrong move.

She shifted, and her warm mouth opened against his neck. Trailing slow, hot kisses down his throat, she took as much as she gave.

He felt her consuming him, taking her time and tasting inch by inch. He was powerless to reciprocate, afraid to move or even breathe. Desperation roared through his body.

When her lips brushed across his nipple, he sucked in a breath. When her tongue made liquid fire rings around his navel, he murmured her name on a ragged breath.

"I want you," she proclaimed, as she wound one silky leg around his thigh.

He was too shocked and needy to protest in any way.

Rising to her knees over him, she licked her lips and gazed at him with such slumberous anticipation that he was ready to spontaneously combust. Then she bent over and took him into her warm hands.

"Susannah," he warned.

But she paid no heed. "Ahh," she said as she stroked his erection and glided fingertips over every slick inch.

Then without warning, she bent her head lower and took his tip into her hot, lush mouth. Sudden electric impulses convulsed along his spine, and he dug his heels into the mattress to keep from jumping out of his skin.

Sweet. Hot. Powerful.

Burying his hands in her thick hair, he issued a low growl and dove headfirst into the sensations caused by her tongue tasting his flesh. When she seduced him even further with deep suction, he got lost inside her desire.

But this didn't feel like simple lust. Everything about it was more complicated, more intense. She was giving him pleasure beyond measure and not asking for anything in return.

"Susannah," he croaked on a harsh breath. "Stop." *Don't stop.*

When she didn't stop—when she only sucked him

in deeper—he gave up. And taking her head in both his hands, he guided her in setting a mind-blowing tempo. The friction was such an exquisite treasure that his heart fell open into her gift.

Whatever she lacked in knowledge, she was making up for with enthusiasm. She wanted to give him pleasure. She wanted so ardently to make it right for him that she'd lost all inhibition.

He could never feel guilty about handing over control of their lovemaking to her—about letting her do all the giving and him the taking. She was making it abundantly clear, with every sexy little sound coming from deep within her throat, that in giving him this night she was also on the receiving end of immeasurable pleasure.

He'd thought he could stop her in the nick of time, and he did try stilling her by issuing a plea. "I can't hold back. Wait…"

But his protests only made her lift her eyes to look at him and then take him in deeper. The expression on her beautiful face wavered somewhere between depthless passion and the absolute certainty of finishing the job she'd started.

He'd wanted her to come with him, needed her to feel the passion as he did, but one look at her ecstasy and he was a goner. No amount of effort could rein him in. It was too intense, too bold.

Vibrating with heat, he jumped over an edge he'd never known he could reach. The whole experience transcended physical and moved into a realm he didn't recognize—someplace magical, nearly spiritual.

Out of breath and sweaty, he hooked his hands under her arms and dragged her up his body. Curling close to him, she murmured something low and settled in as though she expected them to fall asleep in each other's arms.

But that wasn't going to do it for him tonight. Oh, no, there wasn't an ice cube's chance in hell they would be ending things here.

Nathan stirred, dragging her close for a soul-shaking kiss. Mmm. But how could his libido have rebounded this quickly? Susannah had imagined that he would just accept his gift and then give her a few moments to quietly lie in his arms pretending they were lovers for good before falling asleep.

But there was no such thing from him. His musky scent wrapped around her senses, sending her back into a passion that stole her inhibitions once again. There was no time for maybes or dreams of impossible futures—not when a man like this took charge.

His thundering heart beating against her chest told her clearly that he wanted more...much more of her. In a way, it thrilled her to know he wanted her. But in another way, she knew any more of being with him would ruin her forever for anyone else.

With his body so solid and sleek, she had to admit that she was probably already lost. No one else would ever match this man.

Littering her face with tiny butterfly kisses, he moved to her jaw, placing more soft kisses down her neck.

"I've wanted this since the moment we met," he whispered and then moved to kneel between her parted thighs.

For a long moment, he gazed down at her body. The heat from the look in his eyes made her itchy and hot.

While continuing to watch her face closely in the

ambient moonlight, he spread the fingers of one hand over her stomach. The heat seared her right through her nightgown. She gave a silent prayer that he would not take off the gown and look at her not-yet-fully-recovered-from-pregnancy body.

But just then she felt the heel of his other hand gently kneading the place that already ached for his touch. Suddenly she didn't care what he saw as long as he never stopped.

Moaning, she closed her eyes and let the spectacular sensations roll through her body. When she raised her hips, he slipped her panties down and off.

"I want…" His voice was rough, his words barely audible.

She wanted, too. She wanted everything, but her voice completely failed her.

Placing his warm, wet mouth against her stomach, he kissed his way lower. Twitching, she tried hard to hold herself still.

As he slowly slid down her body, he dragged his open mouth over her sensitive skin. A raging fire was building to an inferno inside her as he parted her damp flesh and slid two fingers inside.

"You're so wet," he growled against her skin. "Beautiful. Hot. Just beautiful."

His breath was warm against her skin. "I crave you, Susannah. I need…to taste…"

She stopped hearing anything else. The only sound was the blood rushing through her veins. She grabbed hold of the sheets and held on through a tremendous anticipation.

"Let me…let me…" He lowered his head and opened his mouth over her.

She hadn't known how close she'd been. She hadn't

realized how intense it could be. Her release was long and convulsive, both draining and glorious. She found herself spinning into a place where stars melt and ecstasy resides.

Weeping at the sheer beauty of it, she reached for him, grabbing at his shoulders. "More," she pleaded. "Come with me."

The look on his face was priceless—like a man who'd tasted the best birthday cake ever, but he wasn't quite ready to stop the feast. The sight of his lusty greed added chills to the fever of the moment.

He crawled up her body. "Don't let me hurt you."

"Not a chance." She'd never wanted anything as much in her entire life.

Leaning up on his elbows, he kept his weight off her, staring down into her face as he slowly pushed his way inside her body. It felt like he belonged there—inside her, surrounding her. He stilled, letting her insides get used to his invasion.

Bending his head, he licked her lips, just the barest of touches. Then he raised his head again and smiled the smile of a man who knew exactly what he wanted. She couldn't look away from his deep, compelling gaze. Her mind went blank. Her hips lifted off the bed in some kind of wild, instinctual move. And he slid deeper within her. *Home.*

It was so good, so right.

She wrapped her legs around his hips and squeezed tight. He began moving slow, steady. She raised her head, placed her hands on his face and blindly guided his mouth to hers for a kiss as deep as the feeling behind it. Mimicking with her tongue the actions she wanted him to make with his hips, she telegraphed her longing.

But too soon she found herself once again sliding into oblivion. She tried to hold back, but it was no use.

When she went off, he groaned, stiffened and threw his head back. As her body began convulsing around him, she cried out his name. It was too soon, much too soon. An uncontrollable rush of adrenaline seared through her belly, taking her to such shuddering pleasure that she thought she might pass out entirely.

Oh, my. Gasping for breath, she clung to him as he rolled them both over, keeping her close to his chest. She lay splayed out across his body, sweating profusely while her heart nearly jumped out of her chest.

He recovered faster than she did. Still breathing heavily, he managed to speak. "Are you okay?"

All she could manage was a grunt and a tiny nod of her head.

"I'm sorry that…uh…went so fast. I'd meant for it to last a lot longer."

Those words brought her back to her senses. "Don't be sorry. That was maybe the most breathtaking time of my whole life. Another ten minutes and I'd have been dead for sure."

She couldn't help but chuckle when he relaxed against her and pulled her closer. "I've got no complaints," she whispered. "If you didn't notice, I was right with you hitting the high points. Twice, actually. So, thank you. It was spectacular."

"You're welcome." He placed a kiss against her hair.

It was such a profound moment that she wondered how she could ever hope to live without this man now. She knew she had no choice. Their time was ending before it ever began.

But for now, for just this moment, she could close her eyes and pretend it would last forever.

* * *

Nathan didn't know how long he'd been out. But when he felt Susannah's absence, he opened his eyes to an empty bed. Reluctantly, he turned to the clock and found it had been several hours. How long had she been gone?

Last thing he knew, she was sleeping soundly in his arms. He'd had a moment to wish for things that could never be, for endless nights of the passion they created between them, for as much time to explore every inch of her body, discovering what pleased her and what didn't, as he could stand.

A soft cry sounded in his ears. It was something like the sounds of a small animal in trouble. Sitting up, he swung his feet over the edge of the bed and looked around.

The door to the hallway was standing open. Susannah must've left it ajar when she left. Now that he was awake, he could tell the cries were coming from Melody. Amazing. A mother could hear the call of her baby even through two doors and when she was fast asleep.

It must be an ingrained characteristic of mothers. He wondered if he would ever be able to do the same thing.

Hell, what was wrong with him? He wasn't going to get the chance. Both mother and baby needed to leave the ranch—and soon. The Devotees wouldn't give up easily. Unless he missed his best guess, Samuel would never accept losing Susannah or the baby. Only if the two of them were somewhere thousands of miles away would Samuel ever stop hunting for them.

They were in danger every minute they stayed within the reach of Samuel's tentacles.

Standing, Nathan searched around the room looking for his shorts. When he spotted them in a corner, he slipped them on and then gave a momentary thought to also donning his jeans.

But, no, he wouldn't be going far—just across the hall to check on Susannah and the baby.

He'd peek in to make sure everything was okay and then come back to bed. After he assured himself that they were both fine, maybe he'd be able to sleep or maybe he wouldn't. Either way, he couldn't stand not seeing Susannah one last time tonight.

Sneaking across the hall in the dark, he pushed open her door. A night-light was burning, but it was impossible to see much of the room from his position.

He slid inside and closed the door behind him. Two steps farther into the room and he saw Susannah. She'd propped herself up in bed with a half-dozen pillows behind her back. And Melody was snuggled at her breast.

The sight of them together made his knees wobble. Why hadn't he known all along that this is what he'd been craving? His entire life, since the day his mother died, he'd been desperate for a family of his own. For a loving wife and child who needed him.

And there they were. It was a sight so sweet, so compelling, that he had to ball his hands to keep from reaching out to them.

He must've made a strangled noise of pure need, because at that moment Susannah looked up and spotted him. But she didn't seem distressed to see him standing there.

On the contrary, her smile was reminiscent of a painting of the Madonna. She tilted her head, indicating he should come closer so she wouldn't have to yell at him across the room.

Moving that distance was like wading waist deep in a swamp. His feet were heavy, and his heart was heavy, too. Now that he'd figured it out, how could he let them go?

Susannah patted the bed next to her, and as if in a trance, he climbed right in. The moment he was there, though, he realized she wasn't that comfortable. So he helped her sit forward and positioned himself behind her back.

"That's better. Thanks."

He couldn't say a word. Holding them both felt right. How could he have let so much time go by without understanding that this is what he wanted? These two—in his bed, in his house for good—was what he wanted.

"Why aren't you asleep, Nathan? I tried to sneak out without waking you."

"The bed got cold. I didn't like it alone."

She chuckled, and he could've kicked himself in the head for saying too much. But Lord have mercy, he was in deep. Deep, dumb love. And it had happened fast.

This was different than with his first wife—much different. Back then, he was in love with the idea of being in love. No wonder it hadn't worked out.

But with Susannah, he didn't want to love her. He couldn't possibly be in love with her. The timing was all wrong. The person was all wrong.

Yet here he was, totally and hopelessly lost.

He needed to send them away—for their sakes—to never see them again.

How could he ever manage to do it?

Chapter 9

After breakfast, Nathan didn't go back out on the range with the rest of the hands. Instead, he took his last cup of coffee along with him and made his way to the opposite end of the ranch house to a separate wing where his brother had set up his private rooms.

Nathan seldom—no, make that never—came to this wing of the house. He had no idea what his brother did back in his cavelike rooms. All he knew was that it somehow involved computers and had nothing to do with the ranch. All the ranch's paperwork was done in their offices located in one of the barns.

But today he needed the kind of help he'd hoped his brother could provide.

As he walked, images of last night with Susannah flooded his mind. He would rather not dwell on what they'd done together—not when this morning's errand was to find a way of giving her a safe place to go when she and Melody left the ranch.

Without him.

The images of last night would not disappear from his mind—not ever. They would stick with him for life. But he would prefer to keep them buried until later, maybe years later when the loneliness finally became unbearable and he needed the strength and peace memories of Susannah could provide.

Arriving at his brother's door, Nathan knocked and heard Derek call out an invitation to enter. Maybe today he would finally learn what his brother did with all his time.

He let out a breath and went in. "You have a minute?"

When his eyes adjusted to the low lighting, he realized he was standing in a room that looked a lot like an air traffic control tower. There were computers lining every wall. Lights blinked and buzzers dinged. From another room came various electrical noises, sounding as though a hundred technicians were at work on peripheral equipment in the spare room.

"Derek? Hello?" This first room was unoccupied except by the machines.

In a few seconds, his brother stuck his head out of the other room. "Nathan? For crying out loud, what are you doing here? I don't think I've ever had the pleasure of your company in my office before."

Were they really going to have to deal with old baggage before Nathan could get to the real reason he was here?

"Don't tell me the ranch is actually going to do without you for a day?" Derek grinned, looking so much like their mother that he took Nathan's breath away, and pushed his glasses up on his forehead.

Yep. Looked like at least a few minutes were going to be wasted with talking over ancient grievances.

"I've been up since four-thirty," Nathan ground out. "And I gave the men their working orders hours ago. I'll check on them later, but I needed to talk to you first."

"Well, come in and sit down, then." Derek and his deep blue eyes disappeared into the next room. He was still tall and lanky, and still a pain in the neck.

By the time Nathan made his way over cords and past side tables full of heaven only knew what kind of machines, he found his brother clear across the next room, standing alone in a small kitchenette next to a coffeepot.

"Ready for a refill?" Derek called out.

"No." He lifted his mug in the air to indicate he still had plenty. "But thanks."

"No, problem. It's not every day when the very busy Nathan Pierce deems something important enough to stop work in order to pay his good-for-nothing brother a visit."

Oh, yeah. There it was—the topic that always turned into their biggest hassles and also had become the cause of their last great argument. Nathan regretted calling his brother *lazy* and wished he'd never uttered the word.

But he still believed in the sentiment behind it.

He wasn't sure what to say. So he went to the small round dining table placed in a corner by the kitchenette and took a seat. And he kept his mouth shut.

"Is it bad news?" Derek joined him, placing his steaming mug on the table in front of his place. "It's not Dad's health?"

"To my knowledge, Dad's health is fine. And the ranch is on solid footing now, too, thanks to that influx of cash we got from Samuel Grayson a while back."

"You've still not forgiven Dad for that one, have you?" Derek blew on the coffee. "And by natural extension that means you haven't forgiven me, either. Right?"

Nathan refused to delve into all the bad feelings between them today. "That's not why I've come. What's done is done. But you know how I feel about the Devotees and Grayson. And turns out, it's partially them I'm here to see you about."

"Speaking of Devotees, where's Susannah?" Derek finally took a sip from his mug and studied him over the rim. "She's really something. Has taken up coming to see me at least once a day."

"Susannah has a busy day planned. She's sitting with both the kids this morning and then she'll be working with the horses this afternoon. *She* likes to work."

"Yeah, yeah. I already know what you think of me. But will she be okay? You don't for one moment believe the Devotees have given up on her and the baby. Is it safe to let her roam around the ranch on her own?"

"A couple of the hands will be watching out for her, and I've told her not to go anywhere but to stay close to the house."

"I guess you know what you're doing."

Nathan's temper flared at the subtle dig. "I know better than you. You never stick your nose out of these rooms long enough to find out what's going on in the world. You didn't even believe me when I tried to tell you how dangerous the Devotees were until Laurel was murdered."

Derek laughed so hard he nearly spit coffee all over the table.

"What's so funny?"

"You, bro. You think I don't know what's going on in the world, but it's you who doesn't ever get out past the confines of this ranch. Look around you." He waved an arm toward the myriad of computers and peripheral equipment.

"Computers. So?"

"I get current events from around the world faster than you can blink. Every day I talk to people in New York, China and western Europe. I have information at my fingertips that would take you a hundred years to dig up if you even knew where to look."

Tamping down on his ego for Susannah and the baby's sake, Nathan said, "That's exactly why I'm here. I need... Well, actually, Susannah needs information, and I'm hoping you can find it for her."

Derek sat back in his chair and folded his arms over his chest. "Like what kind of information?"

"Hawk Bledsoe stopped by to see me a few days ago. He says Susannah and Melody need to leave the ranch soon. That they will never be safe while living this close to the Devotees."

"I don't doubt that. So take them someplace. It's easy to see they've come to mean something special to you. All of you go find a safer place."

"You know I can't leave the ranch. I have too many responsibilities to just up and go. Besides managing the ranch operations, there's Sara. I can't leave her, and how could I ever take her with us?"

"I agree that would be tough, but maybe not impossible."

Nathan shook his head, more to convince himself than to convince his brother. "It would be impossible."

Derek sat up in his chair and looked smug. "So maybe I should take Susannah and the baby away myself."

Nathan caught the gleam in his brother's eyes and

knew he was goading him. He refused to rise to the bait.

"Sure thing," he said, letting the sarcasm drip from each word. "But how could you walk away from all this stuff?"

That brought another laugh from Derek. "Are you serious? All the technical equipment anyone needs today can be carried around in a coat pocket and a briefcase. I could be ready to travel at a moment's notice."

Pressing his lips together, Nathan glared at his brother.

"Don't worry. Don't worry. I have other reasons for wanting to stay here, bro." Derek ringed the lip of his mug with a finger. "So what do you want from me?"

"I've been working on cult-exit counseling with Susannah. I'm pretty sure she's got the basics. But a big part of what any ex-cult member needs is a good support system. We've been her support while she's staying on the ranch. But when she leaves, she won't have anyone. I can pay for her physical support almost anywhere she wants to go, but she needs to be around people who understand what she's been through. She needs to keep talking about it on a daily basis."

"I still say you're the best one for the job."

"Derek." He wanted to pound his brother but knew that was an overreaction. "Please? This isn't easy for me."

Derek stared at him for what seemed like forever, saying nothing. "Fine," he finally acknowledged. "I'll start researching group support facilities. I know there's some good ones out there, but I'll need to find one that has experience with cult-recovery counseling."

"Thank you." He stood and took another deep breath,

happy he'd gotten his say and that Derek had agreed to help.

Derek stood, too, and stuck out his hand as though he wanted to shake. "I know this won't patch everything up between us. But maybe it will be a start. At least I hope so."

Taking his brother's hand, he nodded his head and started out the door without saying another word.

Susannah had made him see things in a whole new light.

But before he could go on, he intended to never rest—to never stop trying until he found a way to bring down Samuel Grayson and his Devotees.

After Susannah was safely away, after he was sure she and the baby could never be found, he vowed to call the FBI and offer his services to that end. It was a promise made to himself and his dead ex-wife that he intended to keep—no matter what.

Susannah still felt a little groggy and sleep-deprived after lunch. She'd eaten with Kathryn and Sara while Melody took a nap. But her mind had never left Nathan and the things they'd done last night. She'd spent yet another morning wishing she and Nathan could've talked before breakfast. But he'd said he had too much to do today…maybe tonight.

She certainly hoped so. But she had a feeling they wouldn't get much talking done if they found themselves alone again.

He was too compelling. He was too sexy for her to keep her hands to herself. Their one night had been the best of her entire life, and she wouldn't mind at all doing it over and over.

"Susannah, are you okay?" Kathryn put a hand on

her arm to keep her from leaving right away. "You look tired today. Are you sure you're feeling well?"

"I'm fine. I just didn't get very much sleep last night."

"Not bad dreams of Samuel Grayson again?"

"Oh, no." She didn't intend to confide in Kathryn, though she might've liked to ask her for advice.

She trusted Kathryn—almost as much as she trusted Nathan.

"Kathryn?" Deciding to change the subject, she started on a subject she'd been meaning to discuss. "If anything ever happens to me, would you make sure Melody is well taken care of?"

"What's going to happen to you? You're fine, aren't you?"

She managed a smile. "Yes, of course. I was only wondering. You know, I might be in an accident or something someday. Things like that happen all the time."

Kathryn put her arm around her shoulders for a hug. "Don't think about such things. You're going to live a long life and be the mother of the bride someday."

"But just in case?"

Relenting, Kathryn whispered, "You know I will do whatever is necessary. Everyone on this ranch loves Melody and would die to keep her safe."

"Thanks." That's exactly what she'd wanted to hear.

Susannah told Kathryn she'd see her later this evening when she picked up the baby. Starting off to do her chores in the horse barn, she couldn't stop thinking.

Nathan was planning something, she could tell. He'd probably been trying to find a way to send her away from the ranch without her running into the Devotees. She knew he wouldn't want her to get hurt.

But if she left the ranch, going anywhere, she had a gut feeling the Devotees would find her.

The parade of dead women the police had found, and that Nathan believed had been involved with Samuel, kept haunting her. If she left, she might easily turn into the next casualty.

But that couldn't happen to her child. She refused to let them get their hands on Melody. She would keep thinking and praying on it. But she felt sure Melody would be much better off without her—much safer.

And next to Nathan staying safe, the safety of her little girl was all that mattered anymore.

"It's quitting time, ma'am. Are you ready to call it a day?"

"Not quite," Susannah told the young ranch hand. "But I'll only be just a few more minutes."

"If you'll be okay, then I need to head on out to the bunkhouse and clean up."

"I'll be fine." Susannah flipped her hair out of her face as she felt the sweat beading on her forehead. "Since Nathan warned those Devotees to stay away from the ranch, we haven't seen any sign of them. They wouldn't dare show their faces here again."

"Yes, ma'am. They'd better not." The ranch hand wiped the sweat off his neck with a handkerchief. "Just to be safe, why don't you go over to the ranch office and walk back to the house with Nathan or Mr. Pierce."

"Maybe I will. Thanks for the company this afternoon."

He nodded and strode off, adjusting his gun belt as he walked away. She was sure she wasn't in any danger on the ranch, but Nathan had insisted one of the men keep watch on her at all times when she wasn't in the house.

Having protection was nice, but the whole idea of needing it made her nervous. She had to find a way to leave here soon. Every moment she stayed brought the danger closer to those she loved.

She'd almost come to the conclusion that Melody couldn't come with her when she left. The two of them had to separate—at least for a while. It hurt to think of that, but it hurt worse to think of her baby in the Devotees' clutches.

Perhaps tonight she would seek out Derek and ask him to help her find work in a distant city. He was so good on the internet. He'd told her he had developed several internet businesses that were doing well. The man was a genius. If anyone could figure something out for her to do with her future, it would be him.

She gave the empty stall she'd finished mucking out one last check. Yep...clean as a whistle. She didn't mind the hard work at all. It helped her stop thinking for a few precious hours.

It was time to head back, but she was torn about seeing Nathan. Every time she saw his face, her heart broke a little more. It was crazy to fall so hard for a man who could never be hers for good.

What had she been thinking? Of course Susannah Paul could never hope to keep someone so perfect. Her whole life up to now should've been her first clue.

She was simply not the kind of woman who landed on her feet—never. She'd always landed smack in the horse manure, despite trying so hard to change things.

Kicking at a clod of hay in the main aisle of the barn, she slowly made her way out into what was left of the afternoon sunshine. Shadows were already overtaking the ranch with the coming dusk, but she still couldn't force herself to hurry.

Every moment she delayed was a moment more she could linger in the beauty and majesty of the distant mountains and the idea that she had once belonged to something so special.

She breathed deep, loving the smells of animals and grasses. Turning toward the barn where the ranch offices were housed, she spotted Nathan and his father standing outside the door deep in conversation.

Just look at the man. Her feet froze to the spot while she gazed at his face and her mouth drooled.

Tall and lean, rugged and handsome…he was so special that it made her heart pound.

She couldn't remember a time when she'd wanted anything as badly as she wanted this man. Over the years, she'd trained herself not to set her expectations too high. And Nathan was definitely out of her league.

He and his father were standing toe-to-toe having some kind of serious discussion. It was funny how much they resembled each other. It was like looking into the future and seeing how Nathan would age— pretty darn well if he turned out anything like his father.

Lost in her thoughts, she almost missed a movement out of the corner of her eye. But a sudden chill told her this was something out of the ordinary.

She turned to look and what she saw forced her backward into the shadows of the barn. Three men were coming around the corner of a distant barn. But they were crouching low and staying in the shadows as much as possible.

Devotees. She didn't know them but would recognize the type anywhere. All three of them were beautiful.

Their hair was perfectly combed. Their clothes looking like something out of a Western magazine. Their boots were polished so brightly that you could fix your makeup by checking it in the shine.

And then she noticed the guns—shotguns and handguns. Each man was loaded down with guns.

She watched them as they spotted Nathan and his father, who were still lost in their conversation. One of the Devotees signaled the others to sneak around behind the barn where she was standing and come up on the other barn from behind. Were they really planning on attacking Nathan and his father right on their own property?

Neither of the Pierces was the type of man who would give up without a fight. And because they weren't armed, they would lose the battle today.

That couldn't happen. She couldn't let any such thing happen because of her.

The Devotee men began to split up. They hadn't seen her.

But what could she do? She couldn't just stand here and watch this unfold and not do anything.

Spinning around, she took off at a dead run out the back door of the barn, trying to head off the Devotees before they got too far. This was it. Now was her time.

No one would be hurt because of her—no one.

Chapter 10

As Susannah hit the sunlight, she slowed her steps. What was she doing? Whatever it was, she'd better be smart about it.

Taking a deep breath, she cleared her throat and waved her arm in the air trying to get the Devotees' attention. She was afraid to make too much noise for fear that Nathan and his father would hear and come running.

"Hey, there," she said in as loud a stage whisper as she dared.

That did the trick. All three men turned to stare at her at once.

Her stomach rolled at the sight of their weapons— now pointed in her direction. She wasn't used to seeing Devotees with guns. Only the police in Cold Plains carried weapons. She'd better be a brilliant liar this time. Maybe if she came up with a good enough story she might live through this encounter.

"I'm so glad to see you," she managed in a shaky voice. "Could you give me a ride into town?"

Smile, she reminded herself. Walking toward the man who looked like he might give the orders, she forced what probably looked like a mirror image of the Cheshire cat grin he was wearing.

Fake, but beautiful—just like the caps on this guy's teeth and the contact lenses she was sure he was wearing.

"Are you Susannah Paul? We've been looking for you." The barrel tip of his shotgun lowered to point at the ground.

That made breathing a tad bit easier.

"Yes, that's me. You've been looking for me? Why didn't I know that? I've been stuck out here without a way to go home."

"Didn't you have a baby? Where's the child?"

Breathe. "That's a long story. Poor little thing wasn't born perfect." She shook her head slowly. "Shame. But I couldn't keep her in Cold Plains. Surely you can see that?"

"Where is she?"

"Gone. I shipped her off to a couple in California."

The man speaking narrowed his eyes at her, and the barrel tip inched upward. "Jonathan isn't going to like that."

"Jonathan who? You don't mean Jonathan Miller? What does my baby have to do with him?"

The guy shrugged. "None of my business. He can tell you what he wants you to know when you're back in town. He said bring you both, but you'll have to be enough."

She glanced at the two silent men in the back and shuddered. "Why did it take him so long to send you for me?" That sounded a lot more reasonable than she felt.

"I don't know anything. I just do what I'm told." But he threw her a speculative look. "Why would he tell us to bring the weapons if we were supposed to rescue you?"

Uh-oh. She'd better come up with something fast. "I would assume it was because he was worried that the ranchers would put up a fight to keep me. But if we hurry, we can be gone before they notice."

The gunman glanced over his shoulder and set his mouth in a hard line. "They'd better not make any trouble. Do you need to collect your things before we leave?"

Her things? All she could think about was Nathan and Melody. Come up with something. Get these characters off ranch property and away from Nathan.

"No. Nothing here means anything to me. I have plenty of clothes still hanging in the closet in my room. I can't wait to leave this place and get back there. The sooner the better. It's filthy here. And ugly. I want to go home."

He nodded and grabbed her by the arm. "We'll have to go through the woods. That's how we came in."

"Not a problem. That's how I came in, too."

The farther away from the ranch they drove, the calmer she felt—and the more miserable. She had pretty well sealed her fate by walking out on Nathan and her child.

But the two of them were safe. That thought alone calmed her down and let her brain go to work. If there was any way to survive in Cold Plains, she planned to do it.

All those dead women came to mind. Surveying her companions, the three big men in the car with her, she hoped they were really going to take her to Cold Plains and weren't intent on dumping her body in some ditch.

Screwing up her courage, she asked, "Will you take me straight to my room in the boardinghouse, please?"

"Jonathan wanted to talk to you. He said to bring you to his office."

"But it's late. And look at me. I can't see anyone until I clean up and put on my pretty clothes again."

The driver shot her a disbelieving glance and rolled his eyes. "I'll call him."

Opening his cell, he pushed a couple of buttons, reaching Jonathan on the first try. He explained her request and the reasons for it.

In a couple of minutes, he hung up. "Jonathan says it's okay. I'm not so sure, but he's the boss. He'll stop around to see you in a couple of hours, and the two of you can eat dinner together."

"You didn't tell him about the baby."

"I'm going to let you do that. And if I were you, I'd be ready with a good story."

The way he'd said that made her wonder if he had bought her story of giving the baby away. But if not, why hadn't he told Jonathan? The whole thing was very odd.

The car slowed when it came to Cold Plains' city limits. As they cruised past the lovely houses with the manicured lawns on the outskirts of town, she came to the conclusion she'd better take his advice. There wasn't much time to start thinking up a foolproof story before she had to face Jonathan.

And speaking of that, what the heck did Jonathan

Miller want with her and Melody in the first place? Everything suddenly seemed stranger and stranger. What didn't she know?

Nathan came down the hall, heading for the kitchen and supper. He was eager to see Susannah and the baby. Now, wasn't that a kick in the head? It had been only a few hours since he'd spoken to her for a moment after lunch, but he already missed the hell out of her.

What the devil was he going to do when she left the ranch for good? The ache he'd been trying to force aside crept back into his chest at the thought of never seeing the two of them again.

Hell.

Giving the door to his old bedroom a quick knock before he passed by, he opened it and stuck his head inside. "Susannah? Ready for supper?"

There was no answer. He checked the crib…nothing. He checked the bathroom…nothing. In fact, the shower wasn't even wet. She couldn't have gone straight to the kitchen without cleaning up. She wouldn't.

A tiny niggle of worry started somewhere in the vicinity of his gut, but he dismissed it. There was no reason to worry. Maybe she'd been running late and showered in Sara's suite.

That didn't seem too logical, but he jumped on the idea as a possibility.

Leaving the bedroom, he picked up his steps until he entered the kitchen. But Maria and his father were the only ones there. He wasn't all that eager to see his old man over supper tonight. They'd had another knockdown argument out by the barn this afternoon.

His father didn't want Susannah to leave and had made his point loud and clear. Nathan had tried everything to explain that it was simply not safe enough on the ranch for her and Melody, thanks to those damned Devotees. His father had argued that the family and hands could protect the two of them just as well on the ranch.

At that, Nathan had let loose with his normal tirade about the sale of the property to Samuel Grayson being the cause of all the trouble in the first place.

Things had only gone downhill from there.

"Where's Susannah and the baby?" his father asked as soon as he saw him.

"I dunno. I thought they'd be here." He turned to Maria. "Have you seen them this afternoon?"

"Not me. But I imagine Susannah is still saying good-night to Sara. She just can't seem to get enough of that little gal."

The niggling worry grew. "I'll go over to Sara's rooms and encourage them to come to supper. Susannah needs to keep up her strength." He'd made plans for her later. Well, in his head he'd made plans. And those plans required a second person who was not hungry— at least not for food.

"Yes, indeed," Maria agreed. "Nursing mamas need a good diet." She turned and scowled as she stared right at him. "And plenty of sleep."

He chuckled at her words and headed off toward Sara's. But as he went, he decided that Maria might've accidently come upon the answer. Maybe Susannah had been so tired from their lovemaking last night that she'd fallen asleep at Sara's and Kathryn hadn't wanted to disturb her for supper.

The closer he came to Sara's rooms, the more he became convinced that was what must have happened. So by the time he opened the door to Sara's playroom, he was calm and ready to wake Susannah up with a kiss.

When he opened the door, he spotted the baby right away. She was sleeping peacefully in the little make-shift basket he'd found for her in the attic. But her mother was nowhere in sight.

He didn't want to wake Melody, so he quietly went in search of Kathryn and found her helping Sara out of her play clothes and getting ready for her bath.

"Well, hello, Nathan," Kathryn said with a sweet smile. "Did you bring Susannah with you? I was wondering what had happened to her this afternoon."

The bottom dropped out of his stomach, and his heart clenched. "You haven't heard from her this afternoon at all?"

"No. I just thought she was running late. Don't you know where she is?"

He wanted to run, to start shouting and searching and calling the police.

But he held his place and asked another question first. "When did you last see her?"

"We had lunch together."

He'd seen her right after lunch and had told her about his new rule of having a ranch hand watch over her whenever she was outside the house.

"Can you keep an eye on Melody awhile longer?" He needed to find that ranch hand right away.

"Of course. I wasn't planning on going out tonight. Uh…Nathan." Kathryn told Sara to hold on a moment and stepped out of the little girl's bedroom, obviously needing to talk to him privately.

"Susannah was acting kind of funny this morning."

"Funny how?" He didn't like the sound of that.

"She asked if I would make sure Melody was taken care of in case something happened to her."

"So you think she knew she would be late today?"

Kathryn shook her head. "She wasn't talking about being late. She was talking about forever. I didn't care for her demeanor. She seemed so depressed. And now that she's also missing...well..."

"What?"

"You don't imagine she could take her own life, do you?"

"Of course not." He couldn't think of their time together last night, with her so full of life and seemingly so happy, and accept that she had turned around the day after and committed suicide. "It's not possible."

Someone had to have an idea of where she'd gone. She couldn't have just disappeared.

Susannah wished she could simply disappear, that the floor would open up and she'd fall right through to the other side of the world. Jonathan Miller was at her door, and he had a bouquet of roses in his hand.

Keep smiling. "Come in, Jonathan. Are those for me?"

"They're for you. You look gorgeous. You've lost all the pregnancy weight, and you've gotten a tan. Beautiful."

"Thank you. The flowers are very nice. I'll put them in water." She didn't own a vase, but maybe an empty milk carton would do. "Won't you sit down?"

"If you'll sit with me."

She dumped the roses in the kitchenette sink and joined him in the tiny living room. But she refused to sit too close. This guy was giving her the creeps. She wasn't sure if it was because he was a Devotee and since Nathan had helped her she could see them clearer now or if it was because he was just all around creepy.

Pulling up one of the dinette chairs, she sat across from him. "Can I offer you anything?"

"No, thanks. I was hoping to take you out to dinner tonight, but it's gotten rather late."

She smiled, at a loss for what to say. She hadn't wanted to eat with him anyway. What was he doing bringing her roses?

He finally said, "I understand your child was a girl and that she wasn't perfect. Is that correct?"

Careful. "That's right. It was most unfortunate."

"Where is she?"

Trying hard to look him straight in the eye with a blank stare, she said, "I found a couple on the internet who seemed nice, and they were willing to take her. It was a blessing. I knew Samuel would not have been pleased if I tried to bring her back here, and I didn't want to make any waves in the community. I'm sure she will be much better off where she is."

Actually, Susannah felt positive Melody was a whole lot better off where she was right now—safe and with people who loved her.

"I'm sorry you took that step," Jonathan said with no emotion. "Samuel would've preferred to handle things himself. You know he is always here for your protection. He wants to make life easier for you in whatever way he can. Let him take care of these little life problems."

The hair stood up on her arms. Giving up your child was *a little life problem?* How could she ever have bought into this nonsense?

"Did those ranch people influence your decision?"

Another trick question. "No, not at all. I didn't care

for them. They took me in when I was lost but made me work with the horses in the dirt. It wasn't a pleasant experience."

"I'm sorry you had such a bad time. But you're back where you belong now."

"I'm the one who's sorry if I caused Samuel any concern over my child. I thought I was doing the right thing."

Jonathan smiled, but it still didn't reach his cold eyes. "Samuel forgives you. He has plans for you, Susannah. Big plans. You will be mother to the next generation of Devotees. The child you gave away was not pure. Its father was not a believer. Small wonder it was not sound. Things will be different with the rest of your children. Every one of them will be healthy and perfect."

It was all she could do not to scream at him that Melody was perfectly healthy *and* absolutely beautiful. But the real meaning of what he'd said crawled into her consciousness like a computer virus.

"If I'm to be the mother of perfect children, who will be the father?" Please don't say Samuel. All Samuel's girlfriends ended up dead.

"Samuel has chosen me for that privilege. You and I are to be married. We will make beautiful children together."

Her stomach rolled. "I…see. And when are we supposed to be married?"

"Within the week. But don't worry. Samuel and I will make all the arrangements. I am to be promoted soon—to a place of prominence within Samuel's circle. Becoming my wife will be a great honor. All you have to do is rest and stay calm and do what we tell you."

He reached over as though to take her hand, but she

casually slid it into her lap. "You might want to start back at the gym," he said indulgently. "You're going to be married to the boss soon, and it would be encouraging for people to see you using the facilities."

She nodded as if she agreed with everything he said. What in the world was she going to do? She couldn't marry this horrible man.

Her mind slipped back to the memory of Nathan and how much her time with him had meant to her. Now *there* was a real man…a good man. He was a man she'd not only trusted with her body and her love but also with the job of raising her daughter.

Nathan was so far above the scum sitting across from her right now that he might as well be on the moon while this guy crawled through the gutter.

They were different as heaven and hell.

But she needed to go along with whatever Jonathan said—at least until she could find a way out of Cold Plains. She had no doubt there would be a way out eventually. And she would find it if she kept her eyes open.

Oh, but what would she have to put up with in the meantime? *Stay alive.*

Suddenly it occurred to her that Jonathan might be expecting a kiss tonight to seal their engagement. Eww.

"It's a little late, and I'm not feeling very well," she began.

She'd expected an argument, but Jonathan stood and smiled down on her. "Go to the clinic in the morning for a checkup. Everything must be perfect for the wedding. Your health is the most important thing."

"I'm just a little tired. Surely I don't need to…"

"Susannah. Samuel has chosen me to be your physical guardian. I will be your husband. Your teacher. And your guide in the way of the Devotees. Please do as I say."

Oh, brother. "Yes, Jonathan."

This time he did take her by the hand. "Now, there's my girl. You sleep now. I have an important errand to do yet this evening and should go. But I'll send someone to sit outside to make sure you're safe."

She was under house arrest? And he was running an errand at eleven o'clock? It sounded fishy to her. She almost opened her mouth to question him but realized in the nick of time that a proper Devotee woman would simply accept what they were told. She would have to tread carefully from now on.

She stood to show him out, still praying he would not force a kiss. Whatever was left in her stomach would come back up if he did.

At the door, he turned, and before she could escape, he placed a kiss on her forehead. "We will have a long, fruitful and significant life, Susannah. Pleasant dreams."

And then he was gone. She peeked out the front window and watched him go down the front steps and onto the lighted sidewalk. Finally breathing easier, she remained quietly staring at his retreating back. He hadn't driven; almost no one drove in town. So he must be walking to his errand.

But in a second he stopped in midstride and gazed around as if he was expecting someone to be watching him. Backing up to where she was sure he couldn't see her, her curiosity flared.

What was going on with him? He was acting so strange.

He began creeping down the street as if he didn't

want anyone to notice him. But there wasn't anyone on the street at this hour anyway. It was very odd.

On impulse, she grabbed her keys and jacket and inched out her front door. Where was he heading? If she was going to get out of her house, she had to go now before her guard arrived.

After all, if they were to be married, she had a right to know what Jonathan was up to. Or wasn't that in the Devotee wife's handbook?

Whatever. She couldn't help herself. She had to find out.

Chapter 11

Nate had searched every damned barn on their entire property. He'd done it in record time, too. Barely a half hour had gone by since he'd left Sara's rooms. By now his heart was pumping adrenaline to his body like a gas pedal pumping fuel to a race car.

He was having trouble breathing. And thinking was becoming out of the question.

For the third time, he stopped into the bunkhouse, hoping the young ranch hand had come back from his supper. Sure enough, the moment he walked in he spotted the kid.

"You looking for me, boss?"

Mac must've warned him. "When was the last time you saw Susannah Paul? I told you to stick with her while she was outside the house."

"I did. Honest. All afternoon. She curried a half-dozen horses and then I helped her muck the stalls. She's a hard worker, that one."

Nathan gritted his teeth but held his temper. "Where was the last place you saw her?"

"Just finishing up in the barn. I was running a little late, so I told her to go next door to the office and walk back with you or Mr. Pierce. She said she would."

The ranch hand fidgeted where he stood. "She was fine then, I swear."

What the hell had happened to her between the barn and the office? "What time was this?"

"Near six. It was late."

Nathan shook his head. He'd been there at six—right outside the barn arguing with his father.

The sinking feeling in his gut grew worse. "You didn't see any strangers around about that time, did you?"

The ranch hand straightened up and threw his shoulders back. "No, sir. I wouldn't have let them on the property. Or if I'd spotted them in the woods, I would've notified you right away."

Nathan couldn't be bothered soothing this earnest kid's feelings at the moment. He was too dang worried about where Susannah had gone.

A few of the other hands were still awake in the bunkhouse, playing cards and watching TV. He turned to them and called out, "Hey, y'all, I need your help. Anyone here spot the woman who's been staying with us on the ranch this afternoon? Her name's Susannah. We can't locate her."

A lot of mumbling and shrugging went on for a few moments. But no one spoke up.

"Talk to the other hands, will you? If anyone saw her at all today, I want to know."

"You want us to start a search party, boss?"

He didn't hold out a lot of hope but said, "Check all the barns. I've checked them a couple of times myself. This time go over every inch. If she's injured, she won't be able to call out. I'll call Ford McCall. I'm sure he'll help, maybe organize a few men to search the woods."

Storming out of the bunkhouse into the crisp and clear night air, Nathan was trying his damnedest to stay calm. With his hands shaking, he flipped open his cell and dialed Ford's number.

Ford sounded sleepy, but Nathan couldn't muster the reserve to apologize for waking him. "We have a problem out here, McCall. Susannah is missing, and my gut tells me she's in trouble."

"What? Hold on a second." He could hear Ford yawn and clear his throat. "All right. Say that again."

"Susannah's gone. The baby's here, but the mother's missing. We're searching the ranch, but if you could round up some help, we'll need to check the woods, too."

He couldn't breathe but raced on out of breath to say what he most feared. "I think they may have gotten to her, Ford. The Devotees. Somehow they snatched her right off the ranch."

"Hold on. Calm down. You say her child is still there and safe. But…"

Nathan interrupted him. "Yes, that's why I'm sure something awful has happened. Susannah would never leave her child."

"Well, now, I have big news for you, Nathan. That must've been just what she did. I saw her…early tonight in town. She was getting out of a car and heading into the boardinghouse where she has rooms. She looked happy enough to me. Some male Devotee I didn't recognize right off was driving. And a couple more were in the backseat. She smiled at them and waved when they dropped her off."

Nathan's knees went weak. His brain could not process what Ford was telling him. It wasn't possible. He refused—

"Are you sure it was her? You might've been mistaken."

"No mistake. It was definitely her. I know this is particularly hard for you. Let's hope Susannah comes to her senses."

Nathan's stomach churned, and he hung up the cell without saying another word. Not Susannah. It was impossible.

"Hey, boss. You okay? Are the police coming?"

Shaking his head, he turned his gaze to the same young ranch hand. "No need. She's been spotted in Cold Plains."

Clinching his fists at his side, he spun to face the kid head-on. "I'm sorry I didn't give you a chance before. Apparently she left of her own free will. It wasn't your fault. But I do want to know how those bastards got on and off the ranch without anyone seeing them."

He suddenly thought of Melody. "We'll need to set up a perimeter guard. At least two men should ride the fence line at all times. Armed. And everyone should stay alert for intruders. I won't have those damned Devotees set foot on ranch property again."

"I'll tell Mac, sir." The kid disappeared back into the bunkhouse.

Susannah had gone back—really gone, of her own free will.

With his chin dropped to his chest and his feet dragging through the dirt, Nathan started back toward the house. No one in the family was going to believe this. He didn't believe it. She'd left her baby.

She'd left him.

He wanted to scream…shout. He wanted to find her and shake some sense into her.

Was it his fault?

Or was it something in her background that she'd never divulged that had made the difference? A couple of times he'd known she wasn't telling him everything. Had some dark secret kept her from trusting him?

Was that what happened?

The crushing sensation in his chest made him cough. And the cough caused his eyes to water. Swiping a hand across his face, he sniffed and blew out a breath of air. He wasn't sure he could live through this a second time.

He'd been heading toward the kitchen, but right this moment he couldn't stand to face everyone with the bad news. Where could he go? Was there anywhere on the whole frigging place where he could hide out and lick his wounds?

His feet turned toward Sara's rooms without him being fully aware of the intent. Stumbling forward, his mind filled with images of Susannah—mental pictures of her standing in the sunshine and smiling at him with that special come-to-me look in her eyes…visions of her lying in bed, Melody at her breast, and inviting him to join them broke what was left of his heart.

It had been the most spectacular few weeks of his life. He'd never fallen for anyone so fast and so hard.

Had it all been a ruse? Had she used him?

Considering everything they'd been through, he couldn't find any reason for why she would've done such a thing. He told himself this must be yet another case of Samuel Grayson winning in the end. His hold on Devotees had to be so strong that it was nearly impossible to break free of the bonds he'd created.

Susannah. Susannah.

She was too sweet. She didn't stand a chance with those Devotee sharks. Nothing had changed with them. If anything, things were much more dangerous than they had been when Laurel was there. Oh, God.

He burst into Sara's playroom. It was late, but Kathryn was still sitting on the sofa in a low light.

"Did you find her?" she asked softly.

He could barely breathe again. "She's in Cold Plains, Kathryn. Apparently she'd rather be there instead of here."

"But that can't be. What about Melody?"

The baby. "Where's Melody?"

Kathryn pointed to the other side of the room, where a crib sat in the shadows. "I didn't want to take her back to the house until we found her mother."

He went to the baby's crib and found Melody asleep on her back and looking so peaceful and unaware that it choked him up again. Tears rolled down his cheeks as he gently scooped up the child and cradled her in his arms.

"Don't you worry, darlin'. You're safe here with us."

At least Susannah had enough sense to leave her baby behind with people who would love her and care for her as if she were their own. *Why did she leave?*

"I promise you, Melody. I swear on my mama's grave you will never spend a bad day. I will treat you as though you were my own—more, if that's possible. No family has ever shown a child as much love as you'll get with us on the ranch."

Kathryn came up beside him and put a hand on his

shoulder. "Put her back down now, Nathan. Don't wake the child."

Tenderly, he placed the baby back in the crib and turned to Kathryn. "She'll be all right, won't she? What about feedings?"

Kathryn led him back to the sofa so they could talk. "Susannah left a couple of days' worth of mother's milk. After that, I imagine we can find a good formula. Babies have gotten along on a lot less than this one will have. I'm more concerned about Susannah."

He felt the hurt and rage like a physical blow. "Don't be. She made her choices. Let her deal with it."

"You don't really mean that."

"The hell I don't." He jumped up and grabbed his hat. "If it's okay with you, I'd like to leave Melody here for tonight. We'll work out sleeping arrangements and details tomorrow."

"That's fine. She's no trouble."

He headed for the door.

"Nathan, give yourself a little time. The hurt will fade. But rethink Susannah's predicament. You can't really mean to leave her with those awful people."

"I'll see you tomorrow," he said without turning.

He was suffocating and needed air—lots of air. Maybe for the first time since his mother died, he would take one of the horses out for a midnight ride.

Anything to forget…anything to ease the pain.

Susannah stayed in the shadows as she followed Jonathan through the streets of Cold Plains. No one was out at this hour. Most people in Cold Plains were asleep.

So where was he going for his important errand?

He wasn't headed toward the Cold Plains Community Center. And he'd turned away from Main Street and the side of town where restaurants and clubs might be still open and busy.

Was he going to a secret rendezvous? Did this jerk ask her to marry him when he already had a girlfriend on the side?

That didn't sound much like something a proper Devotee should do. But then sometimes she got the feeling that Jonathan wasn't such a proper Devotee.

The farther away from the center of town they went, the more curious she became. Jonathan was walking into sections of Cold Plains not yet remodeled. She hadn't even known this neighborhood existed.

Houses here were older but not run-down. As she crept down the street, trying to keep Jonathan in sight and not let him know she was following, she came to the conclusion that this part of town must be where the locals lived—the local people who grew up in Cold Plains and hadn't so far decided to join the Devotees.

Before she'd met Nathan, she never thought of those people. Maybe there were more of them around than she knew.

She'd been following Jonathan for almost twenty minutes and was starting to wonder about her safety. They'd left the residential streets and now were walking past abandoned stores and gas stations. When he walked in front of a vacant lot with trees and then turned into some kind of asphalt parking lot up ahead, she took advantage of an old, sturdy pine to hide behind while she tried to see where he was going.

He finally ducked into a building that looked about the size of a small warehouse. She spotted a lighted sign above the door that she had to squint to read.

Jones Brothers Mechanics and Machine Shop. What on earth was Jonathan doing here?

She didn't dare get any closer. What if he came right out and caught her there?

Settling back against the pine, she decided her position here, in the trees next door, could not be spotted by anyone from the deserted-looking building. But with nothing much left to see, her inquisitive mind began going over the various things Jonathan had said, trying to make sense of all this.

Okay, so Samuel wanted her to marry Jonathan and produce babies. She heaved a deep sigh. But why did Jonathan want to marry her?

To please Samuel...well, sure. But what else? What would he gain by having a wife and children?

Maybe he expected to lead a more public life. What had he said earlier about being promoted? He was moving to a place of prominence in Samuel's inner circle. But he'd already been made vice-mayor of the town a few months ago. How much higher could he go?

He could take the mayor's job. But what about the man who was already mayor? What was his name? Oh, yes, Rufus Kittridge. She remembered him. He was a loud, broad-shouldered man with a round face and a huge, toothy smile.

But then where was the current mayor going? She couldn't think of anyplace higher for him to climb. Samuel was the only person who could tell the mayor what to do. The police chief even took some instructions from the mayor.

Mayor Kittridge could be leaving town, she supposed. But according to Nathan, no one left the Devotees except in a box. And what did any of that have to do with a machine shop? It was all very odd. She couldn't figure it out.

After standing there for a full hour, half expecting another car to show up, she figured so much for the idea that this was a meeting of some sort.

So Jonathan was a liar. It was not really surprising. But if he was a liar, what else might he be that she didn't know about? The idea was chilling. No way was she marrying a guy she couldn't trust. He might even be a murderer.

Wishing she could be safe and sound back in her bed with Nathan right now, she started to weep. But that wouldn't help her. She sniffed away the tears, deciding to start being smart and look for any advantage over Jonathan.

Finding out what he was doing inside this building could be one way of getting something on him that would help to free her. However, she wouldn't try moving in closer and get caught tonight.

She might be a little naive, but she was not too stupid to live.

And, oh, how she wanted to live, wanted to be a mother to Melody and a lover to Nathan, wanted a future…away from Devotees.

Getting too tired to stay, Susannah came to the conclusion that she'd found out everything possible for one night. She needed sleep…a few hours at least. It would be easy enough to sneak in the back way to her rooms.

Early tomorrow morning she would come back to this place and find out who owned the building. Someone who worked here would know something about Jonathan. She was sure of it.

* * *

Before first light, Nathan was up and on his way out to the bunkhouse to give the men their orders for the day. He supposed Mac could do this chore for him, but he'd gotten in the habit and doing something familiar this particular morning made him feel almost normal.

The smell of the raw earth and the predawn dew on the hay made him feel normal, as well. He loved it here…always had.

What a bad night. He'd tossed and turned for a few hours and then had taken his third cold shower in as many hours.

He still didn't understand. Maybe he never would.

Susannah had claimed to love the ranch as much as he did. And the look in her eyes said she loved him, too. He felt as sure of that as anything in his life.

In fact, her love had changed him in their short time together. He'd been on the verge of becoming an angry old man before Susannah, untrusting and miserable. Due to her influence, he'd forced aside his old issues with the women in his life and learned to trust again.

Had she wrecked all that in one moment?

He thought of trust, and then of her walking away, and stopped in his tracks. What the hell had he been thinking? He trusted her—absolutely and irrevocably.

That meant he also believed in her. She would never let him down…just like she would never leave on her own accord—much less abandon her child.

He took off toward the bunkhouse, hoping Mac would be there. When he arrived, the men had assembled.

They looked at him with something like pity in their eyes—all except for one guy who pushed his way toward the front.

"Boss, I heard you'd wanted info on that Paul woman's whereabouts yesterday afternoon. You still interested?"

His heart jumped in his chest. "What did you see?"

"I was in my old pickup on my way over to Grainger to stay the night with my girl last night. And running late, so I was…ah…going a little too fast. But I passed up a sedan that had a funny look to it. You know, too slick and new looking for a car from 'round here. More like something those new Cold Plains folk would drive."

Nathan nodded and prayed the guy would hurry up with his story.

"Well, the lady was in the front seat. But that wasn't the strangest part. The really odd thing was the two guys in the back both had shotguns laid out across their laps."

"Shotguns? You sure?"

"I got a good gander from the cab of my truck as I passed them. Thought it was funny."

Funny as a cold slap of reality. "Thanks," he told the guy. "Mac, can you handle the ranch today?"

"Sure, boss. Where are you going?"

"There's something I have to do. I'm going into town."

"You in need of backup?"

He wouldn't risk any of his men, not if the Devotees had a stash of weapons.

"No. But thanks. This is something I have to do alone."

He owed it to Susannah for doubting her. And if it took everything he had, he would get her out of that town. Or die trying.

Chapter 12

Susannah bolted out of bed before dawn. Feeling cranky and more curious about Jonathan than ever, she skipped breakfast. There wasn't anything in her kitchen anyway, and she didn't dare go out to eat in Cold Plains.

The more time she spent around real Devotees, the better the chance of one of them noticing that she seemed different than before, not the same as they were. She *was* different now.

She crept to the window and checked out the street. No sign of any guard. What she felt like doing was going back to the ranch for some of Maria's good cooking...and to cuddle Melody...and for another night with Nathan.

But since none of that was possible, she needed to find a way to make it possible. Of course, she knew if she just called the ranch that someone would come for her. But that wouldn't be safe—not for the people she loved and not for her. The Devotees would only come for her again, and the next time someone would die.

Nathan could not die for her sake. They might as well kill her right now. She also didn't want anyone to know about Melody's presence on the ranch. The Devotees seemed to buy her story about sending the baby away. She wanted to keep it that way.

So her best bet still had to be Jonathan. There was something smarmy and not quite right about him, and she was determined to find out what. If she learned anything terrible, she would turn him in to the police. If it was only something embarrassing, she could try threatening him with exposure to make him help her escape from Cold Plains for good.

Wondering what she might find out was driving her crazy. Did she have to wait until business hours to go back to that mechanic's shop? Pacing her room like a wounded mother tiger, she wondered what the heck Jonathan had been doing there at midnight.

Oh, the heck with it. She'd go now. Maybe someone would come to work early so she could talk to them.

She locked her door and took a deep breath of the crisp morning air. But it didn't smell nearly as good here in town as it always had at the ranch early in the morning. Where was the clean cedar smell she so loved? Where was the odor of hay and horses that she'd grown fond of over the past few weeks?

Making her way back to the mechanic's shop took a lot less time than it had following Jonathan there last night. Still, she tried not to run. She didn't want to draw attention to herself.

Dawn was nearly breaking, and one or two people were already out and about, probably on their way to work. Things seemed so normal here. But now that she could see the reality of the Devotees, she knew an evil lurked around every street corner.

She tried not to feel the oppressive truth in each breath and thought instead of Nathan and Melody. Wonderfully warm thoughts, they brought her back within minutes to the same spot as last night.

Hesitating under her pine, she gazed at the mechanic's shop. It looked exactly the same in the cold, gray morning light as it had last night. Nothing had changed. No cars were parked in front of the place yet. It looked as though none of the employees had come in early.

She settled down to wait for someone to arrive. After a half hour, she wondered how smart this idea really was. What if she was walking into some kind of criminals' den?

Just about to give it up as a bad idea, she straightened, gathered herself and got ready to leave. But then she heard a door opening. Spinning to the sound, she saw Jonathan coming out of the shop. And he was carrying a package under his arm as he locked the mechanic's door behind him.

Suddenly nervous, she found a better hiding place in the vacant lot where she could watch what he did and not be spotted. But he didn't do anything. After locking up, he casually walked away, going in a slightly different direction than he'd come last night.

She let him move about a block ahead before she hastened to follow him. The gray light of predawn was giving way to brighter and brighter daylight, and she had a hard time staying out of sight. But Jonathan didn't seem to be worried about being followed, because he never turned to look around. He kept up a steady pace...not running but not strolling, either.

He seemed to have a specific destination in mind.

After another block, it was apparent that he was heading for the community center. Man, that place gave her the creeps.

Remembering what her friend had said about strange things going on in a hidden basement, Susannah wasn't eager to even set foot in the place again. When he arrived there, Jonathan did another odd thing. Instead of entering the center through the front or back doors as everyone else always had, he went across the empty parking lot and entered through a side door she hadn't noticed in the past.

Slowing her pace to a crawl, she located another shadow, this one coming from both the two-story building across the street and the awning covering a storefront. She stood still, trying to decide what to do. Feeling temporarily hidden well enough to escape detection from anyone across the street—at least until the sun was high in the sky—she spent a moment looking up at the huge three-story structure of the community center, marveling as she always had at its beauty.

Samuel had spared no expense, using the money he'd made from selling his fake healing water to build a monument to himself. White columns, marble walkways and perfectly landscaped grounds made the center a showplace.

As she stood quietly gawking at the construction and wondering what she should do next, a fancy silver-colored car drove up and parked in the blacktopped lot nearest to the side door. Samuel got out and went inside. Before she had time to consider what the heck he would be doing at this early hour, a pickup pulled up and the chief of police, Bo Fargo, climbed down and quickly made his way inside by using the same side door.

Susannah absently wrapped her arms around her body in a protective move.

Her breathing started coming in little bursts just as another car drove up—this one a big black sedan, and a man she thought she recognized as Rufus Kittridge, the mayor of Cold Plains, got out and went inside. She remembered the mayor with a warm, easy smile, but he wasn't smiling much this morning.

Some kind of big meeting must be going on. She'd say a town council meeting, but it seemed a strange time.

A few more men arrived within minutes, some walking and some in cars, and all of them looked like important Devotees. Interesting. Secret dawn meetings?

But it didn't seem to her as though she'd come across anything useful to her situation. She didn't have the nerve to actually go inside the center and see what was going on.

She wanted to go back to her room but was afraid to move a muscle, afraid of getting caught spying.

Just as she thought it might be safe to run, the side door opened and Jonathan came back out into the parking lot, still carrying the same package. Now what could he be up to?

This time, he did look around as though searching for anyone who might be about. Susannah moved deeper into the shadows. He didn't appear to notice her, and no one else was anywhere to be seen.

Then Jonathan got down on all fours and slid his whole body under one of the cars like a mechanic might do. Weird.

But he wasn't there long. In a few moments, he was back out in the lavender light of dawn—but without the package.

Before she could gather her wits and figure out what he was up to, he moved to a different doorway, one a little farther away. She had to squint to see what he was doing.

He'd apparently needed to contact someone, because he pulled a cell phone out of his pocket and began making a call.

"Wait up, son."

Nathan turned to see his father coming his way. Irritated at the delay, he threw his hands on his hips and made it clear waiting for his father was an imposition.

He needed to go to town…and to go now.

When his father finally arrived at his side, Nathan shook his head. "I'm in a hurry. No time to talk."

"Mac tells me you're thinking about heading into town this morning on a fool's errand. I want to know what you think you're doing."

"None of your business."

"Where's Susannah this morning?"

Dang his father anyway. "If you already know what I'm doing, then why'd you ask?"

"'Cause I thought I might've misunderstood Mac. You can't seriously be going to town on your white horse to rescue the fair maiden?"

Damned nosy old man. "Susannah didn't deliberately leave the ranch of her own free will. The men who took her had shotguns. Does forcing her into a car with weapons drawn sound like she wanted to go along with them?"

His father scowled, and a deep skeptical noise came from his throat. "Of course she didn't go willing. Unlike one idiot I could name, I never thought she did."

Nathan's anger flashed fast, the same way it always

did when he talked to his father for more than five minutes. But this time he didn't have time to finish the argument.

"I'm leaving. Save it for someone who cares."

His father held up his hand and moved close enough to throw a punch—but he didn't. "Hold on. Hold on. I don't know why talking to you always brings out the worst in me, son. But I do know now that selling that creek land to Grayson was a terrible mistake. I truly thought it would be good for the community. That the new people and new construction would be a boon for the whole town."

"Some wonderful boon."

"You're right." His father heaved a heavy sigh. "We were better off poor and miserable. I know that now. But I can't take back what's done.

"What I *can* do," he added quickly, "is see to it my youngest son doesn't die for my mistakes. You can't go chasing after the girl alone. They'll cut you both down before you make it back home."

"Watch me. Those bastards don't scare me. I have a better chance alone. If I take some of the men, it'll be tougher getting into town. The Devotees will know something's up. Once I'm there, Samuel won't dare bring out the guns in the middle of his pristine city and ruin the image he tries so hard to create. But I'll be carrying a .357 Magnum under my jacket. And I intend to call Hawk and the FBI as soon as I find Susannah. She will live through this. I swear."

"I've grown fond of the girl myself." His father's tone softened. "And she damned well ought to be where she wants to be. With her child. And with us."

Nathan shook his head again, but this time it was to say, "I told you so." "I'm leaving. Get out of my way."

"Wait." His father put a hand on his shoulder. "At least be smart enough to take me with you. I get your point about a posse of men storming the town. That would only cause more trouble. But I can't sit here on the ranch worrying over your welfare."

He pulled a .45 out of his jacket. "I'm armed, too. Let me help, son."

"Get in the truck." Nathan didn't want to think too much about the things his father had said. But he knew he would—after he had Susannah safely back at the ranch.

A couple of minutes later, they were on the road. "Did you hear the whole story of what happened to Susannah?" he asked his father.

"Why don't you tell me what you know?"

He could hardly stand for his father being so reasonable. What had caused this huge change in the man?

Later… This was not the time.

"It seems some of those bastard Devotees sneaked onto the ranch right at quitting time last night. I didn't realize it then, but apparently Susannah was still in the horse barn alone. A hand said she told him she would walk back to the house with one of us."

"Quitting time? Around the same time when you and I were talking outside the office?"

"Arguing, you mean? Yeah, I'm thinking that was the same time."

Downshifting, Nathan tried not to let what he was saying blind him to his driving. "Apparently the Devotees managed to overtake her without either of us hearing a thing."

His father fisted his hands in his lap. "We weren't whispering."

"No. We never do."

"Things will change between us from now on." His father exhaled and looked down at his hands.

"Why?" Had he really said that aloud? Well, in for a penny... "Why will things change? What's different, Dad?"

"Don't you know? Are you really so blind? Susannah's what's changed. She's made a big difference—with all of us."

Nathan knew he felt different around her. But was that a permanent change of some sort? And what did his father mean when he said "all of us"?

"How, Dad? How did she change things for you?"

His father cleared his throat. "Well, now, I guess that's hard to pinpoint exactly. But she's a very special woman. After just a few minutes of talking to her, I found myself spilling my guts. Said things to that girl I hadn't even said to myself. Should've, though. Should've said some of those things to you, too."

"Like what?" His own voice sounded so raspy, he could barely hear himself talk.

"Like how when your mama died, I blamed myself for not being there for her when she got sick. Or how I'd let my father-in-law run me around half the countryside doing errands for the ranch and neglecting my ailing wife. After she passed away, I told him what I thought of him and his damned ranch. Bastard cut me out of his will and left everything to your brother."

What? That couldn't be. "I always thought he didn't leave you anything because you didn't love the land. At least not like Grandpa and I did."

"Think about it a moment. Your grandfather knew how much you loved the ranch, Nathan. So why didn't he leave the whole place to you? 'Cause he was a vindictive schemer, that's why. He didn't want me to have control, so he left it to the one person who couldn't have cared less. The one person you wouldn't fight."

His father took a breath but kept talking. "The old man knew damned well I couldn't let the ranch go to hell. Knew I would hang around for the rest of my life and run the place, though it will never legally be mine."

"That doesn't sound like Grandpa." Truthfully, it sounded more like something an evil person like Samuel Grayson would do.

"You never really knew him, son. He only let you see one side."

Nathan drove on quietly for a few minutes, not sure of how to take what he'd just learned.

"But then you do care about the land?" He felt a little like a twelve-year-old, begging for attention from a father who was so obsessed in his own grief that he couldn't be bothered with either his youngest son or the ranch he loved.

"When I married your mama, I knew I was marrying her family's land, too. She loved this place and wouldn't ever have wanted to be anywhere else. And I loved her. That we were going to live and work this ranch was a given. The surprise came when her old man wouldn't give up an inch. He constantly tested me, seeing just how much crap I would take to prove I cared about the family's land."

His father stared out the window at the miles of range and woods passing by the window. "I put up with him for her sake at first and then for yours. After my beloved Sallie passed away, I wished I had gone, too. Nothing interested me. I'm afraid you were a casualty of that time, son. Your grandfather used you against me, somehow in his mind getting even with me because she had died and I lived. I can't tell you how much I regret that now."

The lump in Nathan's throat threatened to choke him. He needed time to process all of this. When he'd freed Susannah from the Devotees, he would take some time to consider everything he'd learned today.

After a long silence, his father asked, "Do you love her?"

He couldn't pretend not to know who his old man was referring to. "I don't know." But that was a lie. "Maybe I do love her. But she will never be safe on the ranch as long as Samuel Grayson and his Devotees are right next door in Cold Plains."

"What do you intend to do about that?"

"What can I do? She and Melody will have to go away, someplace so far that Samuel Grayson will never be able to get his evil hands on either one of them."

His father opened his mouth as if to say something more. Then he closed it again and turned his head to look out the windshield as the outskirts of Cold Plains came into view.

Out of the corner of his eye, Nathan saw the older man fingering the .45 stuck in his waistband. Damn. Why hadn't he thought about his father being hurt before he'd started out?

It was too late now for regrets and recriminations. He would just have to be smarter and quicker than any of Samuel Grayson's Devotees and henchmen.

No one could get hurt today. He refused to allow it—not his father and certainly not Susannah.

He loved her. Now that he'd finally admitted it to himself, he had to make sure she lived long enough to admit it to her, too.

* * *

The minutes were ticking by for Susannah as she kept inching around, staying in the shade of the store's awning and out of the direct sunlight. After Jonathan had made his phone call, he'd disappeared back inside the community center.

Everything was peaceful as the sun began to rise in the sky. In another twenty minutes, the streets would be full of people—Devotees and locals alike all going to work or to shop.

She'd been racking her brain for some kind of answers. But she still hadn't come up with a decent reason for what she'd seen Jonathan doing.

Was he a mechanic in his spare time? She'd thought long and hard and had finally remembered that the car he'd been under belonged to the mayor. Had he agreed to fix the mayor's car?

Hadn't he said he was currently the vice-mayor? Perhaps he'd agreed to fix his boss's car during the meeting.

That didn't sound like Jonathan. For a Devotee, he seemed much too self-absorbed to be doing favors for anyone.

What else had he said while he was bragging about himself last night?

It was something about moving up. But the only place up from vice-mayor was the mayor's job.

Suddenly something she'd remembered from an old TV show came to mind. She hadn't watched TV since she'd come to Cold Plains. But before, when she'd been stuck in crummy motel rooms waiting for Melody's father to finish his dirty "businesses," she'd had nothing to do but watch old reruns and movies on TV.

On several of the old cop shows, the bad guys would

blow up a car in order to get rid of their enemies or rivals. Was that what Jonathan had in mind?

Her nerves started jumping. Oh, my goodness. As crazy as it might be, it almost sounded like a reasonable explanation for what she'd seen.

Darn. What should she do? If she went to the police chief and told him this story and it turned out not to be true, she could be in even bigger trouble with the Devotees. Then they would know she didn't believe and wasn't a good little Devotee anymore.

They might kill her right away.

But she couldn't let a nice man like the mayor be killed, could she? And she sure as heck didn't know the first thing about car mechanics. She would only end up either discovered and outed as an imposter and liar—or blown up with the mayor.

Neither one of those options sounded good to her.

How about Ford McCall? Yes, she could probably go there for help. Nathan had been positive the lawman was not a Devotee. And she trusted Nathan's opinion above all others.

Oh, Nathan, what should I do?

She would give anything to be able to ask for his advice. But Nathan wasn't here.

Thank heaven. He was safe at home with Melody and his family.

This was all up to her.

She had to find Ford. But where should she look? At the police office? His home? It was early yet.

Darn. Darn. Darn. She couldn't think fast enough.

Just then, the community center's side door opened once again, and Mayor Kittridge strolled out. He stopped, gazing around in every direction. He looked like a man who had done something wrong and didn't want to be caught. Then he tried staying in the shadows of the building as though he didn't want anyone to see him while he went to his car.

Susannah's feet started moving before her mind caught up. He didn't know. She was sure of it.

Pretty soon she was running full out, hoping against hope to head him off.

"No! The car! Stay away from the car!"

Chapter 13

Running and screaming at the top of her lungs, Susannah prayed she'd make it there in time. Devotee or not, the mayor was a kind human being and didn't deserve to die like this.

"Stop!" she screamed. "Mayor Kittridge, turn around!"

Sprinting faster than she figured was humanly possible, she kept going and passed the car, holding her breath. "Go back. The car…the car…"

It took another minute or two to catch up to the mayor.

"What's the matter with you?" He gazed at her through narrowed, disbelieving eyes. "Do I know you? Stop that screaming."

Out of breath, she gasped for air and tried to explain. "Something is wrong with your car. Some…someone did something to it."

She grabbed him by the shirtsleeve. "Please, come away. Don't go near it."

"Are you having a breakdown? You're a Devotee, aren't you? We mustn't let ourselves become so out of control, dear. Remember…"

"Now!" She began dragging him in the other direction.

"Please," he said as he jerked back on his arm and tried to stand his ground. "I have to leave. Someone is waiting for me. Don't make me call the chief of police."

Using all her strength, she dragged him a few more feet. "No time to explain. Go ahead and call the police. From inside the center! Please just come with me."

"What on earth is wrong with you, young lady? I…"

She dashed around behind him and gave him a big shove. The confused man was off balance and went to his knees.

"That does it," he yelled. "Stay away from…"

The entire world suddenly crashed in around them, and Susannah got lost in the chaos—dark and black.

The explosion rocked Nathan's pickup and shocked him enough to make him slow down. As soon as his ears stopped ringing, he looked over at his father.

"You okay, Dad?"

"I guess so. What the hell…?"

Throwing the truck in Park, Nathan opened the door. "Can you handle driving? I'll do better on foot. I've got to find Susannah."

"I can drive. You think she'll be somewhere close to whatever that explosion was?" He nodded toward the column of thick black smoke rising to the sky about three blocks away.

"Hope not. Only one way to find out."

"Good luck, son. I'll drive the truck as close in to the trouble as possible and wait to hear from you."

Nathan took off, running flat out toward the smoke. *Please don't let that involve Susannah.* Things in Cold Plains didn't just blow up. Something bad had happened.

The farther into the center of town he ran, the more he realized the smoke originated from somewhere near the community center. He couldn't imagine any reason why Susannah would be anywhere close to the center. At least he prayed she wouldn't.

The Devotees hadn't forced her to undergo some ritual, had they? If she was hurt, they would regret it.

His heart pounded. His lungs screamed for air. His brain burned with horrible images.

If Susannah died, he would see to it Samuel Grayson paid with his life. Nathan's own life wouldn't matter.

As his feet beat against the sidewalk pavement, he found himself surrounded by more and more people. Everyone wanted to see what was going on.

Darting out into the street, he figured dodging one or two cars would be a whole lot easier than the hordes of onlookers. But then a car honked behind him.

"Hey! Watch out! Out of the way." The voice came from the car.

He turned and saw Ford McCall in his police cruiser, trying to drive toward the scene. Spinning, he grabbed hold of Ford's passenger door handle and jumped into the front seat.

"What the hell are you doing here, Nathan?"

"Susannah—" That was the only word he could manage.

Ford turned on his siren and concentrated on driving as fast as possible through the throngs of people. "You have any idea what happened?"

Out of breath, Nathan shook his head.

"But you think Susannah had something to do with it?"

Wheezing past the dry throat, he answered, "She better not be anywhere near there."

"But you think she might be." It wasn't a question.

Good thing, because Nathan still couldn't utter a sound.

As they turned a street corner, he spotted his worst nightmare straight ahead: a huge column of smoke coming from a burning car in the community center parking lot.

"Holy hell." Ford steered to the curb, threw his cruiser into Park and shut it down. "We're on foot from here."

Before climbing out of his vehicle, Ford called in and asked for fire department assistance. Nathan was way ahead of him—dashing through the crowds, pushing, shoving, not bothering to excuse himself. He forced his way closer and closer.

Finally at the ring of people nearest the blazing car, he drew in enough air to ask, "Was anyone in there when it went up?"

"That's the mayor's car!" someone shouted.

"Can't tell if he was in the car from here," another man called out.

A siren sounded in the distance, but it was coming closer. He had to find Susannah. If she wasn't in the car, was she being held inside the center?

He backed away from the still-blazing car and all the people standing around it. Looking up at the center, he spotted a side door that no one seemed to be guarding.

If he could reach it, maybe he'd be able to slide inside for a look around the place.

The crowds were swelling with onlookers, but he found a way to skirt the worst of them. He flattened himself to the bushes next to the wall of the center and tried to remain invisible behind the fog of smoke as he headed toward the side door.

Before he was close enough to try the door handle, he spotted someone sitting on the sidewalk about ten feet from the door. And that someone was holding her head in her hands. When the smoke lifted some, he knew immediately it was Susannah.

Thank God.

Bending to one knee beside her, he asked, "Are you hurt? What can I do?"

"Nathan? Oh, Nathan."

"I'm here. Is it bad?"

"Mayor Kittridge. Help him."

"Huh?" Nathan looked around and found a pair of men's shoes attached to legs and sticking out of a flower bed.

He didn't want to leave Susannah. "Is he dead?"

"I don't know. Jonathan Miller tried to kill him."

Reaching for his cell phone, Nathan straightened and went to check on the body while he waited to be put through to Ford. He bent beside the still, prone body of the mayor and checked his pulse. Thankfully, the man's pulse was strong and steady.

Ford came on the line. "McCall."

"I'm standing near the side entrance to the community center. The one closest to the parking lot. Mayor Kittridge has been injured. Susannah's here but hurt."

"I'll call the Cold Plains Urgent Care Clinic to send an ambulance and paramedics."

"I don't want Devotees touching Susannah ever again." He walked away from the mayor, satisfied the man's breathing was easy, and went back to be with her. "She told me Jonathan Miller tried to kill the mayor."

"I just saw Miller in the crowd. He won't get far."

"Susannah may be hurt bad. There's a lot of blood."

"Take her to the new doc's place. Doc Black. Corner of Success Avenue and Principle Lane."

"Where?"

"Used to be Oak and Elm. In a converted 1930s bungalow. I'll be there as soon as I can clear things up here. I need to question Susannah."

Not bothering to acknowledge him, Nathan hung up and bent to speak to Susannah. "The mayor's alive. Paramedics are coming for him. How badly are you hurt?"

As she dropped her hands, blood spewed all over her blouse and jacket and then sprayed his jacket, too.

"Oh, crap, sweetheart. Why didn't you say something?"

Nathan ripped his jacket off and tore open his shirt. In seconds, he'd made a compress for her wound. "Hold this tightly against your forehead. We're going to find Dr. Black."

"But…"

He lifted her and cradled her in his arms as he would a child. "Hang on. This won't take long. Try to stay still."

No one paid any attention to them as he charged through the streets past the crowds of people with Susannah holding on to her head with one hand and on to him with the other. She was losing so much blood. Deep waterfalls of the stuff gushed, soaking through his shirt in seconds.

Racing down the last street, he saw Rafe Black coming the other way.

"Dr. Black! It's Susannah. Look at all this blood. Help her."

The doctor reversed course and ran alongside him. "Is she conscious?"

"Yes. Just talked to her. But there's so much blood."

The doc let them inside his office and asked Susannah to lie down, keeping her from becoming too lightheaded. "Let me take a look."

With a quick wash of his hands, Dr. Black was bending over her with cotton swabs.

His own hands were empty and itching to help. Fidgety, Nathan didn't know what to do with himself. He paced around the office, needing something to do but not wanting to move away from her side.

"Lie still, Susannah," the doctor was saying. "There's a large chunk of metal embedded in your forehead. It's deep but looks a lot worse than I think it is. Still, head wounds bleed like a son of a gun."

Nathan stepped to the doctor's side. "Is there anything I can do to help?"

The doctor shook his head. "I'll get the bleeding stopped in a minute or two. After I give her something to numb the area, I'll try debriding the wound so I can clean up the jagged edges, then suture whatever I can. No guarantees how pretty it's going to be."

"I don't care about that. Will she be all right?"

"She'll live. Just give me some time here." He never looked up but went on with his work.

Nathan stepped right outside and took a deep breath. He felt nauseous and shaky but fought it off.

His father. He'd almost forgotten.

After punching in his father's number on his cell,

he told him where he and Susannah were and asked him to join them. Then he lifted his head and sniffed the air. The smell of burning rubber filled his nostrils. That was going to be one hell of a mess for someone to clean up.

What the devil had gone down here? And how had Susannah ended up in the middle of all the trouble?

By the time his father pulled the pickup to the curb in front of the doctor's office, Nathan was sitting on the front steps, trying to make some sense of things.

When he explained everything to his dad, there were still big pieces of the puzzle he hadn't figured out yet.

"Best bet is to wait until Susannah can shed light on what she knows," his father told him.

"Ford's on his way. He wants to talk to her."

"We'll sit in on that discussion."

Yeah, they would—whether Ford liked the idea or not.

"Are you okay, son? You look a little pale."

"I'm fine. But I have to say I never want to live through another scare like that in my lifetime."

His father patted his knee. "That's just the way life goes. When we love someone, their welfare becomes more important than our own. You may have to hold up under a lot more of the same kind of stress or worse before your time on this earth is over."

It was a good half hour later when Ford arrived. By then, the smoky scent in the air had dissipated and his nerves were back under control.

"Nate. Mr. Pierce. Everybody okay here?"

"We're good. But I'm not sure about Susannah. The doc is still working on her."

"Miller got away before I could reel him in. I put

out a BOLO on him. He won't get far. We have a lot of questions. For Susannah, too."

Nathan's father got to his feet. "Well, let's check on the doc's progress."

The three of them entered the office with Ford in the lead. "Doc Black?"

The doctor came out of the inner office. He ignored the fact his white coat was covered in blood spatters.

Taking a breath, he said, "I'm giving her a few minutes to rest. She's going to be as weak as a newborn for a day or two. But I don't believe she lost enough blood for a transfusion. She's in good health. She'll rebound."

Nathan's knees started to wobble again, but his father quietly held him up from behind. "Can we see her now?"

"In a minute." Dr. Black turned to Ford. "Were there any other casualties? Is a doctor needed anywhere else?"

"The only other person hurt in the explosion was Mayor Kittridge. But I just talked to the Devotee clinic and was told he'll be fine. Had a few minor cuts and bruises and a slight concussion but no broken bones. He claims he'll be back to work by tomorrow."

The doc nodded. "What the hell happened?"

"That's what we hope Susannah can tell us."

"All right. Let me check on her a second." Dr. Black went back into the interior room.

But he was back within minutes. "She's sitting up and drinking orange juice. I think she should be able to answer questions now."

Nathan was the first to reach her side as she sat on the edge of an examining table. She seemed fragile, and the bandage covering her forehead looked ominous. He wanted to gather her up in his arms and race back to the ranch, where he could protect her and keep her from any further harm. But he knew that wouldn't happen for a little while yet.

"How are you feeling?" he asked.

"Oh, Nathan." She reached out her hand to him.

He took her offered hand in his own and entwined their fingers. Her skin felt warm, soft. The jolt of love he experienced with her touch was a big surprise. But maybe it shouldn't have been.

"You're going to be just fine," he said with a hoarse voice. "Can you talk for a few minutes? Ford needs to ask you some questions."

Never letting loose of his hand, she turned first to his father. "Hi, Mr. Pierce. Did you and Nathan come together? In the same truck?"

"Yes. We came to bring you back home where you belong. Didn't know you were going to be caught up in an explosion, though. Wish we'd gotten to you first."

She smiled and Nathan's heart stuttered. "Thank you." Then she turned to Ford. "Did you find Jonathan? He can't get away."

"He won't." Ford nodded his head and took out a pocket recorder. "He's not in custody yet, but it won't be long. Can you tell us about what you saw?"

"It's kind of a long story."

"Are you feeling strong enough to tell it? And do you mind if I record what you have to say?"

Susannah's cheeks blushed, and she squeezed Nathan's hand. It was such a sweet gesture, and she looked so innocent and beautiful that he fell more in love than he'd ever been.

"Um…I guess not. But will any of the Devotees—or Samuel—have to hear it?"

"I have a strong suspicion Miller will be tried in

either the state or federal courts. So, no, probably none of the Devotees will ever need to hear this recording."

"Okay. Can I just tell it from the beginning?"

"Sure. Start when you're ready."

Dr. Black cut in. "Don't overtax your strength, Susannah. If this is going to take more than a few minutes, maybe you should do it tomorrow."

"I'm okay. Really. And there's one part Ford needs to hear."

Dr. Black nodded and backed to the other side of the room, standing by in case she needed his help.

"I guess maybe you already know that three Devotees, men I didn't recognize but knew were part of the group, came to the ranch yesterday carrying big guns," she began. "I saw them sneaking up to ambush Nathan and his father. But I knew they were really there for me."

Nathan's blood pressure soared. He had been so wrapped up in arguing with his father that he hadn't noticed a thing.

"So I called out to them and told them a story," she went on. "I said I'd been wanting to go back to town and asked if they would give me a ride."

Nathan cleared his throat.

She glanced up at him. "Well, I couldn't let them hurt you, could I?" Turning back to Ford, she said, "I also told them that I'd given Melody away."

Saying her daughter's name apparently broke some kind of dam within her. She turned back to Nathan with tears in her eyes. "Is the baby okay? Kathryn has her?"

"Kathryn is taking good care of her. Melody is just fine. But I bet she wants her mama to come home."

For a moment, Susannah looked like she might explode in tears. Nathan braced for the worst. But after biting her lip for a second, she returned to telling her tale.

"They seemed to believe my lie about Melody. Looking back, I guess she wasn't the real reason they wanted me, after all. Just a few hours later, Jonathan showed up at my place, claiming the two of us were to be married. He said it like it was a fact I should simply accept. According to him, Samuel wanted things to be that way between us."

"Did he attack you? Lay his hands on you? Hurt you in any way?" His temper flared, hot and fast.

Ford held up his hand to keep Nathan quiet. "Let her finish, Pierce."

Nathan had to grit his teeth and clamp his mouth shut. He was still holding her hand, or he might've punched a wall.

"He only kissed my forehead, Nathan. Thank goodness. I played along with the marriage idea like I was a good little Devotee. But something just didn't feel right about Jonathan. He seemed—uh—odd, I guess. So when he left my place on foot at eleven o'clock at night, I followed him."

"You what?" Nathan took her by the shoulder. "Don't you know how dangerous that was? What if something happened to you?"

The look in her eyes almost took him to his knees. "It's all right. I know, sweetheart." The way she said it was like a secret communication between them, telling him she understood how much he cared. "But *nothing* happened."

Turning back to Ford, she continued her story. "Jonathan went to a mechanic's shop on the outskirts of town. He never spotted me, but he stayed there so long that I got tired and went back to my room to bed."

"Thank God."

Ford ignored his remark. "Could you find the place again?"

"Oh, sure. I went back there this morning."

"What?" Nathan was stunned. "Why would you do such a thing?"

"I was hoping to catch Jonathan doing something embarrassing or illegal. Anything I could use to trade for my freedom. I thought if I found out something terrible about him, he might help me sneak out of town without Samuel ordering my execution."

"Do you have some kind of death wish?" Nathan's fury came up to bite him once again. He began storming around the room.

"It was all I could think of, Nathan. I didn't know what else to do."

This time Ford cleared his throat and forced Susannah's attention back to her story. "So what happened this morning?"

"I watched as he came out of the shop right before dawn. I guess he might have been in there all night, because he was still in his same clothes. I followed him again. This time he was carrying a package and went to the community center."

She stopped talking and looked around for the juice box. After taking another sip, she went on. "Quite a few other Devotees arrived after he went inside—including Samuel, the police chief and the mayor. But then, as I was wondering what was going on at that hour, Jonathan came back out with the same package and slid it under the mayor's car."

"Under the car?"

"Yes, just like a mechanic would. I thought maybe he was fixing something under there. But then I remembered that he'd said he was coming into a promotion soon."

"A promotion? To what?"

"He didn't say. He'd been claiming to be the vice-mayor. I got to thinking that would have to mean he expected to become the mayor."

Ford actually coughed before he got his composure back. "Why didn't you call me?"

Susannah blushed again. "And say what? I didn't know anything. Not for sure. Still, I was about to go look for a phone when the mayor came out of the center and started walking toward his car."

"And you tried to warn him off?" Nathan exploded, so full of fear for her that he couldn't contain himself. "You ran toward the danger to save a damned Devotee? They'd just as soon kill you as look at you."

"He's a human being. And supposed to be a pretty nice guy. Did you want me to stand there and watch him die?"

"That does it. We're going back to the ranch." He turned to Ford. "If you want more from her, come out tomorrow. I'm taking her home."

"Careful, Nathan. The Devotees are busy with the explosion for now. But they won't stay that way for long."

"Let 'em come. *This* time we'll be ready."

Chapter 14

After sleeping most of twelve hours with the only interruptions to feed Melody and to eat a little something herself, Susannah woke up rather the worse for wear. But it didn't matter.

The aches in her bones, the slight deafness, the itching wound under the bandage on her forehead...none of it mattered. She was back in a place where people cared about her.

Not only did they care but they'd actually worried about her when she'd left. They were worried enough to come after her. She tried hard but couldn't come up with any other time in her life when she'd felt so welcome.

It was killing her to know her time here was growing shorter. Only a matter of a couple more days, not even a week, and then she would have to take Melody and disappear. Otherwise, the Devotees would get to her—somehow.

And people would be hurt in the process—*people* like Nathan. He'd been the biggest worrier. She'd seen it in his eyes when he'd listened to her story.

He cared. He really cared.

She still wasn't entirely positive that he was in love with her, but the fact that he had worried and wanted to protect her made her feel all warm inside. Wishing she wasn't so much in love with him, she could see that the only thing for her to do was to leave him. He would be safe.

Her life would never be the same after this—after him. That was for sure. But perhaps if she left soon, he would be able to move on to have a good life without her. Maybe he could forget and find someone to love who wasn't so screwed up.

That thought made her queasy. The idea of Nathan with someone else was heart wrenching. But it was far better than having him hurt due to her hanging around too long.

She just needed to force herself to make plans for where to go and what she and Melody could do with the rest of their lives. It would not be easy, but it had to be done.

Crawling out of bed, she checked on the baby and was surprised to find Melody already awake and quietly lying in her crib, looking around. "Good morning, Miss Sunshine. You look happy. Are you glad to have Mama home?"

Melody made a gurgling noise that sounded like "ahgoo."

"Very nice, sweetheart. Just wait until I tell Nathan that you're already making real sounds. He'll be so happy."

Susannah checked Melody's diaper and reached for

a dry one. Her little girl was almost six weeks old now, and she watched her mother's every move intently, following her with big curious eyes.

She smiled down at her precious baby while finishing her change and she was surprised when Melody smiled back. That should have pleased her even more. And as a proud mama, she was happy. But despite her joy, big sloppy tears began running down her cheeks.

Without Nathan, she would have no one to share all the small milestones her child reached, no one to share the anxiety when worrying about her little girl as she grew. The loneliness became overwhelming.

Dumb. She wiped her eyes and sniffed the tears back. She'd been alone virtually her entire life, even when she'd been surrounded by family or a supposed lover. It shouldn't bother her in the least to continue on that way. In fact, now she had someone. She had Melody. The two of them would be the family she'd always wished she'd had.

And she had better get busy with finding a way for the two of them to survive.

She scooped up the baby and strolled to the kitchen, trying to memorize every wall photo and floorboard on the way. This place would have a special space in her heart, and she wanted to remember it and Nathan always.

"There you are." Maria's smile was so big it covered her whole face. "Are you hungry?"

After returning to the ranch yesterday, Maria had shoved food at her every hour or so until it was bedtime, claiming she *looked hungry.* "I think I'm still full from yesterday, thanks. I've never seen so much food at one time. It was all great. But right now I'd love a cup of tea or decaf if you've got it."

"Coming right up."

"After that, will you be able to take a quick trip into town?" The deep voice from behind her sent shivers down her spine—very pleasant shivers.

"Good morning, Nathan." She turned and he was there.

He bent and kissed Melody on her forehead. "Good morning to two lovely ladies." As he was straightening, his lips came within a millimeter of hers, and she held her breath, hoping for her own kiss.

Smiling, he gave her a peck on the cheek. Then a slight frown crossed his features.

"I know going back to Cold Plains today may be difficult," he began, "but Ford would like you to point out that warehouse you told him about. We'll stay on the outskirts of town and should have no trouble keeping away from most of the Devotees."

"Have they caught Jonathan yet?"

"Not yet. But Ford wants all the evidence he can gather when they do."

"Okay. But Melody has to stay here. Just in case."

Nathan nodded. "Of course."

"The baby smiled back at me when I smiled at her this morning."

"Really?" Nathan held his arms outstretched. "Let's see if she'll do it for me."

She turned over her little girl and watched as he began cooing at the baby. Her heart thumped and ached. Here she was, once again wishing for a lifetime with this man—wishes that were as worthless as a snow shovel in the desert.

Nathan tickled Melody under the chin and smiled at her. The baby smiled right back and made a "goo-da" sound.

"Look at that," he said with amazement. "She's trying to talk."

"Oh, shoot." Susannah couldn't stand here and watch while the two people she loved more than anything grew closer, knowing they would soon have to separate. "Excuse me a moment."

"Are you okay?"

"I'll be right back." She made a dash for the bedroom before the waterworks started again.

This was crazy. She was such a wimp. How was she ever going to leave this place and keep her head high when the time came?

Ford brought his cruiser out to the ranch to pick them up for the run into town. Nathan was grateful for the small attempt at disguise for Susannah's sake. The trip was quick and relatively painless.

Susannah pointed out the pine tree she'd stood beside while she watched the warehouse. Ford took a line of sight measurement and then about two dozen photos. When he was done, he mumbled something about needing to find a reasonable judge to issue a search warrant for the place.

When they returned to the ranch, Maria had the table set for a four-course midday dinner and insisted they eat every bite. After all the food, Susannah asked if she could visit with Sara for the afternoon. And as much as he wanted to spend every waking moment with Susannah himself, how could he say no?

He needed to ride out and check on Mac and the men anyway. It had been a couple of days since he'd turned the reins over to Mac, and he was sure all would be running smoothly. Still, he would feel better if he saw for himself.

A few hours later, his cell rang. When he answered, it was his old buddy Hawk on the line with real FBI business.

"Thought you should know the Wyoming Highway Patrol stopped Miller just outside of Green River. They have him in custody in Cheyenne. There're a couple of things I'd like to talk to you about if you have a moment."

"Give me a half hour, and I'll meet you at the ranch office. I'll tell security you're expected."

They clicked off and Nathan headed back, wondering what Hawk would say.

"How long can you keep up this much security?" Standing outside near the office, Hawk asked the question as he gestured to the ranch hands who had escorted him in from the highway.

"As long as it takes."

"Better make that sooner rather than later, bud. You need to move that gal and her baby off the premises. At least for the next few months."

"What do you know?"

"I know Samuel Grayson is getting antsy. Somehow he seems to know the law is closing in on him. And having one Devotee try to kill another hasn't helped. If anything, he's tightening up his security and becoming more paranoid."

"Have you found out anything about Miller's background? Who the hell is that guy?"

"First off, it seems Miller is not his real name. His fingerprints say he's a guy named Winchester with U.S. Navy SEAL training and a demolition specialty. But he was busted out of the service for a fragging incident. He tried to kill a senior officer. Unfortunately, he escaped the brig and went on the run. He thought becoming a Devotee would make a great place to hide out—until he got greedy for power."

"So he never was a true believer?"

"Nope. But then I'm not so sure Grayson believes that crap he spouts, either. And that Miller-Winchester dude is not the only Devotee who's handy with weapons and ready to use them under Grayson's orders."

"What is the FBI really doing about Samuel—secretly?"

Hawk sighed and ran a hand through his hair. "We're running a task force from nearby. Intend to nail that creep."

"Nearby? Where?"

"A cabin in the woods." Hawk grinned. "I've got three agents with cabin fever on my hands. But we're making a little progress. I've decided our best bet is to find a Devotee who can get us inside information. Someone like Susannah Paul, for instance."

Nathan opened his mouth to tell him what he thought of that idea, but Hawk cut him off. "Down, boy. She can't go back there now, I know. But I'm still looking for one of them who's becoming disgruntled."

"I want to help. I have exit counseling training that might be useful." Wow, where had that come from?

Hawk shook his head. "Your job is to take care of the residents, both human and animal, here on the ranch. All of your people need to stay away from Cold Plains and the Devotees. Send your men to Laramie for supplies. Besides, Nate, you have too many responsibilities right here. What we're doing is far too risky."

Despite his initial frustration, Nathan quickly had to admit Hawk was right. If he was free to do whatever he wanted, he would be whisking Susannah and the baby off to safety and certainly not running to a cabin in the woods to join the fight.

Life wasn't always fair.

"One last thing, bud. I will say this again because it's important. Get that woman and her baby off this land and send them far, far away. Now. Within the next forty-eight hours. Having them here may become a huge distraction that Grayson can't ignore, and I can't battle a deadly distraction right now. I want him quiet and unsuspecting while we run this sting."

Nathan nodded but didn't say a word. He knew they were out of time. But damn, how could he possibly stand to send them away when he'd only just discovered how much he loved them both?

Another day was gone too soon, Susannah thought with a heavy sigh. Everyone was already in bed. The house was dark and silent.

Not really hungry or in pain, she just couldn't sleep. She stood, vacantly staring at the inside of the refrigerator, daydreaming about Nathan.

She hadn't had time to be alone with him at all today, and he had headed off right after supper. But she was well aware of how short their time was and knew he felt the same. She could feel the tension between them growing.

This afternoon, she had sought out Nathan's brother and begged him to speed up his search for somewhere she and Melody could go to be safe. She fervently hoped it would also be a place where she could earn a living for the two of them.

Derek had looked at her a little oddly but then said he'd been tracking down a place and he'd tell her all about it tomorrow. She had a day, maybe two, left. It had been everything she could do to gaze at Nathan over the supper table and not explode in tears.

And now she wanted him so badly she was becoming detached—unfocused. Her body craved his touch. Her mind felt desperate to hear him speak.

"Still hungry?"

She spun to the sound of his voice, hoping she was not dreaming. She was hungry for something, all right.

"I just can't sleep."

"Me neither. Are you in pain?"

Shaking her head, she poured herself a glass of cold water and shut the refrigerator door. "I feel remarkably better. Maybe tomorrow Dr. Black can come out and remove the stitches."

The water trickled down her dry throat, but she still felt hoarse and tense. Just look at the man standing there…gorgeous…rugged and so sexy he made her whole body hum.

Naked to the waist, his jeans were unbuttoned and the zipper halfway down. The stubble on his jaw was dark and made him look almost dangerous. Her mouth watered. Her fingers flexed, compelled to touch. She put the glass down before she dropped it.

His eyes darkened, and she knew he was thinking the same thing. He wanted a kiss and probably a lot more. This desperation could be cooled only one way. But she was terrified to move—frozen to the spot from fear he would turn her away.

They both knew she would be leaving soon. And Nathan was not a love-'em-and-leave-'em kind of guy. If it came to that, neither was she—except she needed one more stolen night with this man.

He shook his head slightly as though he was arguing

with her or maybe with himself. Then he said softly, "I need you. Now."

Thank God.

He moved closer—close enough that she could feel the heat of his hard body just inches away from hers.

But the nearer he came, with that special look in his eyes, the more her body turned to mush. Her bones liquefied, and she could barely hold up her head.

Reaching out to steady herself by hanging on to him, she opened her mouth ever so slightly. Trying to drag in desperately needed air without letting him know, she thought she might die in another moment if he didn't hurry up.

Just when she was sure he would never make a move, he murmured, "I…" He looked so frustrated and annoyed that she almost stepped back. "I can't be gentle tonight. I need you—too much. Is that okay?"

"Very okay."

She barely had the words out of her mouth when he scooped her up and turned, dashing down the hall to the guest bedroom. He kicked the door closed behind him and lowered her feet to the floor. But she couldn't have moved if her life depended on it.

Apparently neither could he. He leaned in, pinning her to the door, and opened his mouth over hers, taking this seduction to another level. It was a level they'd never reached before…to something so hot that it sizzled and burned and nearly choked her with all the female hormones raging through her body. She felt her own climax beginning and forced it back. Not yet, please not yet.

Never breaking the kiss, he ripped at her nightgown and panties until they were mere shreds on the floor. As he lowered his jeans, he managed to touch her everywhere. Desire burst through her veins and rocked her backward.

Moments later, he reached the spot between her legs and groaned. "Wrap your legs around my waist."

With both hands, he held her bottom and helped her into position. Hot, wet and light-headed, she wasn't sure how this would work, but she didn't care.

He pushed her back against the door and entered her in one quick thrust. She tilted her hips, and he drove deeper. Her head was swimming as she held her breath.

"Don't move," he said through gritted teeth.

She understood the sentiment and would've loved to comply—to make this go on and on. Trying to still, she opened her eyes and looked up at him.

His jaw was tight, his eyes were half-closed. His face full of desire—for her—was a sight she would love seeing again and again.

But this was her last chance, her last opportunity to revel in the feel of him inside her and focused solely on her pleasure.

"Susannah," he breathed.

That clinched things. It was impossible not to grind her hips against his. She felt her own body betraying her—her internal muscles tightened around him, pulling him in.

He grabbed her around the waist and began to drive into her, moaning and cursing under his breath with the effort to hold back. But it was too late for that.

In a blur of thrusts, deeper and deeper, he plastered himself to her. Someone screamed. Her? And she called his name. Begging, pleading, she reached for that edge and dragged him along with her.

The climax hit her like a tornado, whistling in her ears like a marching band and surging through to her core, shaking her to her soul. It took her to that elusive spot…to the stars.

He bent his body and brought his mouth down on hers, swallowing her gasps and cries. With one last thrust, he brought his head up and growled, low and deep.

His climax took her over that edge again, and she joined him in one last drenching explosion.

For moments afterward, they tried to catch their breaths. She knew she couldn't have moved if she'd wanted to. But she didn't want to. She wanted to stay right here, sweaty and out of breath, forever.

"Wow," she finally whispered against his neck. "That was…that was…"

"Amazing," he finished for her. "I can't believe I never even made it to the bed."

"Didn't hear me complaining."

Carefully backing up, he shifted his hold on her and carried her to the bed. As he laid her down on her back, he murmured, "Give me another shot at doing it right?"

She'd give him another shot—or twenty or maybe a whole lifetime.

How was she ever going to manage her life from here on knowing what she knew now? They were so good together. They were perfect, in fact.

Swallowing the first sob, she smiled up at him. "We have all night."

It was their last night.

Chapter 15

Out of breath again, Nathan gazed down at Susannah and couldn't believe his good fortune. She was amazing. They'd been making love pretty much nonstop for the past few hours. He knew he could go on with this forever, but she must need sleep sometime.

He rolled over, taking her with him. She curled into his side and buried her face in his shoulder.

Looking at the ceiling, he let his pounding heart settle. He'd planned to say a few things to her tonight when they were alone. But words never seemed quite adequate while he was inside her and everything in the world was all right.

Perhaps after they both caught a little sleep would be a better time to talk—assuming he could keep his hands off her long enough.

Closing his eyes, he gloried in the wonder of holding a woman like this one—a woman he loved and who he knew loved him in return.

But then he heard a heartbreaking sound that pulled him wide awake with a thud. "Susannah, what's wrong?"

She sniffed into his shoulder. "Nothing."

"Oh, no, you don't." He sat up with his back to the headboard and dragged her along with him.

He'd heard her cry ecstatic, lustful tears earlier and knew the difference between then and now. "After what we've done together tonight, you and I should be able to say anything to each other. 'Nothing' is not much of an answer. Something is bothering you, and you owe me an explanation."

His first impulse was to believe he'd done something wrong, not been good enough. Or maybe he somehow managed to hurt her despite how careful he'd tried to be.

But when he flashed back to the past few hours and the many times she'd come for him, at least twice for every one of his, he erased those fears. These tiny sobs were sad, emotional sounds.

"Are you hurting because you and Melody will be leaving soon? I can understand that. It makes me miserable, too, but can't we talk about it?"

"We haven't talked much," she finally mumbled. "Not really. Not about things that matter. Of course I'm unhappy about leaving. But…but…I can't go and not tell you how much you mean to me. How much I love you."

The words startled him even though he'd guessed the truth days ago. This would be a good time for him to say those same words back to her. But he wondered if that wouldn't make things infinitely harder on her. Wrenching her away from a man she knew loved her beyond measure seemed unnecessarily cruel. So instead of pouring out his heart, he remained silent. But he put his arm around her and drew her closer to his chest, protecting her always—even from his love.

"I know," he mumbled. "Still, I'm not sure you trust me."

"You're a fine one to talk about trust," she said through the sniffles. "You don't trust that I love you enough. Do you? Is that because of your ex-wife?"

"That's not fair." Man, now he was sounding like a twelve-year-old again.

"All right." He sighed when she folded her arms over her chest. "I have had a few issues with trust over my lifetime. Starting when my mother got sick and promised me she would be well enough to go to my grade school graduation."

"Is that when she died?"

He nodded, though he wasn't sure she could see him in the dark. "Three days before graduation. I never went. Her funeral was on the same day."

"Oh," she said softly and put her head on his shoulder. "I'm sorry."

Now that he'd said that much, he was on a roll. "And then my sister promised me faithfully she would never leave the ranch. That we would be buddies forever and take care of each other for good. We might each get married, but we'd bring our spouses to live on the ranch. No one would come between us."

"Did she say that when you were both little? Right after your mother died?"

"Yeah. And it wasn't long before she was riding off on the back of some guy's motorcycle. She couldn't be bothered with the ranch or even her own child." *Or with her promise to me.*

"And then your wife left for the lure of Cold

Plains. I can see how that would make it hard for you to trust me."

"Not you." He wanted to say *all women,* but that wasn't strictly true. "Well, not lately. I've had a problem with trusting anyone. But since you've been here you've made me see things differently."

Well, he'd had that one relapse when he discovered she was back in Cold Plains, but now might not be the time to discuss it. He knew the kind of panic he'd experienced that night was a thing of the past.

"So it's not that I don't trust you," he added quietly. "I do. But now that I know you well, I can see you've been holding back. Not telling me everything. You know my faults."

He laughed softly. "Pointed most of them out to me. But I don't know anything at all about yours. Or your past before you took off with Melody's father. I think you're the one who doesn't trust."

"Oh, but my background isn't important. Not like yours. It doesn't mean anything." Her whole life didn't mean much when she thought of it.

The only thing Susannah felt she'd ever done that made a difference in this world was Melody. And as much as she loved her little girl and would die for her, she'd been an accident—not something Susannah had wanted or planned.

She'd stumbled into the best thing that had ever happened to her…typical.

"Stop that."

"Stop what?"

"Stop putting yourself down. You always do. Like you think you're not worthwhile or something."

"No, I don't do that."

"Sure you do. Putting yourself down was what made you vulnerable to Samuel Grayson. You believed that he could make you a better person. When actually you're a thousand times better a person than he is or ever will be."

"But…" Was that true? When she really thought about Samuel, maybe it was.

"And I have a feeling that same attitude is what led to your going off with a drug dealer you barely knew and getting yourself pregnant. You don't believe you have anything to offer someone decent. But the truth is you have so much to offer."

She wanted to complain, to tell him that wasn't true. But then she thought back to the person she once was— before Nathan. Was that really the kind of person she'd been then?

"I… Maybe you're right."

"Tell me who you are—or were," he demanded in a gentle tone. "Why don't you have a family somewhere who can help you?"

She'd tried hard to forget, to deny her past. When she became pregnant and found Cold Plains, she'd been determined to change. Funny… By giving her life up to Samuel Grayson's lies, she hadn't changed at all.

She did owe everything to Nathan and his family. And though she hadn't told this story to anyone ever, she should tell him. He deserved to know what kind of person he'd been harboring. He'd made all the difference in her life, and he wouldn't know that unless she told him why.

"I suppose my mother and father are still alive— somewhere. But they wouldn't help me to a drink of water if I was dying of thirst. I'm not sure I could even find my father. Or would want to."

She drew in a breath and let it out. "Worse yet, I'm not positive I know my father's real name. He ran out on my mother and me right after I was born.

"Crazy, isn't it?" she added. "Melody's father didn't even stick around for that long. I thought I was in love with a man who turned out to be just like my father, when I'd always sworn never to do anything so stupid."

But that wasn't the worst. *Lord, give her the strength to tell him all of it.* She owed him that much, even knowing he would probably look at her with disgust from now on.

Nathan didn't say a word. But he took her hand in his and locked their fingers, giving her strength to go on.

"I don't know why my father took off. It doesn't matter now. But my mother always blamed me. In her wildest ravings, she claimed they were happy until I came along. She said I was a terrible baby, crying all the time and sickly. And that I cost too much money to keep. And that's why he'd left."

Closing her eyes, she saw the first image of her mother that she could ever remember. A tall, cold woman, screaming about how terrible and no good a child she was, right in front of the neighbors.

"I worked hard to stay out of her way. I learned how to become a shadow when she was around. Still, if I needed her to sign a report card or give me permission to take a field trip, I usually ended up afterward in a crawl space in the attic, curled up so I could become invisible."

"I'm sorry," Nathan whispered. "How did you survive?"

"By believing what she said. I didn't need anything because I was worthless. Everyone else got lunch money. I ate their throwaways. That was good enough for me. Other people had friends, but I didn't deserve such luxuries."

She didn't mean to make her past sound so pitiful. It was bad, but others had it a lot worse. She hadn't wanted to tell him the whole story at all. But she'd gone this far and couldn't find a way to stop now. *Please don't let him turn his back when I'm done.*

He squeezed her hand. "Didn't you have any teachers who noticed your situation? No one who paid attention?"

"My mother remarried when I was in the second grade. To a career army man. Her treatment toward me never changed, but from then on we moved from place to place a lot. I never got to know my teachers well enough for them to see what was going on. I wasn't smart or particularly bad. I was easy to overlook."

"I'm surprised you didn't run away from home."

"That's what a strong person would've done. Or a smart person. I wasn't either one. Besides, my mother had two more kids with my stepfather and didn't treat them any better than she'd treated me. I was pretty useless, but I couldn't leave my little brother and sister on their own, could I?"

"But you did. Eventually."

"No." She almost smiled at her stupidity. "They left me. I'd just turned nineteen when my stepfather accepted a transfer to Germany. I couldn't be counted as a dependent, so I couldn't go."

"They left you behind?"

"It wasn't so bad. At least I didn't have to hear about how stupid and worthless I was from my mother anymore. I did worry about the little kids, though, for a long time. But in a few weeks I was struggling so hard to survive that I stopped worrying about anything."

"What…" His voice was rough, low. "What did you do?"

"The only thing a girl with no training and no schooling could do." Here it came: the worst of it. "I walked the streets."

When Nathan didn't say anything or even move, she wondered if he would hate her now. "I didn't last long 'cause I wasn't very good at that, either. I never enjoyed the company of men. Not until…you.

"And anyway, I almost starved to death," she went on hurriedly. "Only managed a month or two until Melody's father offered to take me in. He was on the road a lot and needed someone to…uh…be around when he needed a woman to take the edge off."

"The drug dealer? Was he also your drug dealer?"

She took her hand back and bit her lip before she answered, "I never did drugs. I couldn't afford them, and he didn't want a meth head as a companion. Before I met him, it was all I could do to find food and a place to sleep."

That explanation seemed a bit harsh. Of course Nathan would think the worst. Why not? So had she.

"I suppose if I hadn't gotten pregnant with Melody, I probably would've gone the drug route eventually. It's one way of forgetting your circumstances."

"It's one way to kill yourself, too."

"Sometimes dead is better."

She could feel the tears welling up again. Would they never stop? She swiped frantically at her eyes and begged them to go away.

"There you have it," she said through pursed lips. "My story. Now, aren't you glad I'm leaving?"

Nathan reached over and turned on the bedside light. The light was low, but it was more than she wanted right now.

"Don't," she said with a strain in her voice. "I'll go back to the bedroom and Melody. But don't look at me. Not now."

She swung her feet over the side of the bed, turning her back on him and wondering what had happened to her clothes. She would hate to have to ask to borrow a shirt in order to make it back to her room. But she couldn't go across the hall stark naked.

"Susannah." He spoke so softly that she almost didn't hear him.

But then he was standing right in front of her. "Look at me." He put his hands on her shoulders and moved closer.

She didn't want to face him, didn't want to see the disgust in his eyes.

But she loved him enough to die for him. So she did as he asked and lifted her chin to look up at him.

The man was an amazing specimen. Standing there, it was easy to see he was tough but gentle. She hoped he wouldn't hate her forever.

"Your story doesn't make you sound worthless or stupid," he said, gazing down at her with a tender look in his eyes. "It makes you sound like a survivor. I'm glad you told me. I've been frantic about you and Melody having to leave the ranch, worried the minute you left us behind you would become vulnerable to some other bad guy. Now, I'm a little less worried."

He knelt before her and gazed into her eyes. "I dread the thought of you leaving, darlin'. I…"

His eyes filled, and he shifted his head as if to shake

it off. Amazing. The man was so tenderhearted. The sight of him worrying about her ripped at her heart.

Her eyes filled again, too. "You've saved me from more than the Devotees. I don't feel worthless anymore. You made me feel beautiful—and almost capable. Now I can believe I'll be a good mother to Melody. And that's all your doing. We'll be okay. Thanks to you."

He shook his head more forcefully now. "You did that by yourself. I only showed you one way to be different than you were. You took the ball and ran with it."

"I'll never forget you, Nathan. Not ever." She leaned her forehead to his—unwilling to walk away from this wonderful man.

But she knew it was time. Everything had been said. If she was selfish and grabbed another extraordinary day with him, it could put him in danger.

He leaned in and covered her mouth with his. She poured her heart and soul into the kiss.

As the heat began to take them away to that incredible place they'd found together, she tasted salty tears. But when they broke apart to take a breath, she couldn't be sure whose tears they'd been.

Oh, Lord, how would she ever do without this man?

The next morning dawned with her back in her room alone—except for Melody. She was going to have to learn to live with that from now on.

Today was the day she must find a place to go and prepare to leave. If she could, she'd like to be out of here first thing tomorrow. Determined but miserable, she dragged her heels getting herself and Melody dressed for the day, knowing the minutes were ticking away.

When she carried Melody into the kitchen, only

Maria was there making breakfast. "There you two are," she said. "Sit yourselves down at the table, and let me wait on you."

"Just tea and maybe a piece of toast for me. Melody has had her breakfast."

Maria set a mug of tea and a plate of biscuits and honey on the table in front of her. "Mind if I join you for a minute, honey?"

"Please do." She dug into the food. She hadn't thought she was hungry, but no one made biscuits like Maria.

"I wanted to say something before you leave," Maria began. "You should know we'll all be sorry to see you go. You've made a big difference around here—a *big* difference. And you'll be sorely missed."

Her hand stilled with the mug in the air as she tried to smile. "Thanks, Maria. But all of you were doing fine before me. You'll get along just as well when I'm gone."

"No, we won't, sugar." Maria patted her arm. "Before you and Melody came, this place felt like a grave-yard. Everyone went around with their chins dragging to their chests. Hardly anyone talked to each other. Oh, Nathan and Mr. Pierce would yell sometimes. But no one said anything important. We weren't really living. Just existing. I don't know what we'll do when you're gone."

It was the most she'd ever heard Maria say at one time.

Susannah had to swallow hard to speak. "I'll miss you, too. But you know why I have to go."

Maria stood up and pushed her chair under the table. "It don't seem fair. All that talk about being a better person and those Devotees are anything but."

She fisted her hands. "I've got work to do. I can't be

sitting around waiting for everyone to show up whenever they please. Mr. Pierce is the only one not fed yet. If he shows up anytime soon, tell him to help himself." With that, she stormed out of the kitchen.

The next bite of biscuit stuck in Susannah's throat. She'd lost her appetite.

"These are good people, Melody." She turned to her baby in the convertible car seat Mr. Pierce had bought for her. "Maybe someday we can come back for a visit. I want you to get to know the people who saved your life."

Taking a sip of tea, she listed the steps in her head that she needed to take to find a way to leave. First off, she would seek out Derek. The last time she'd seen him, he'd said he was onto something. Then she would spend some time with Sara and Kathryn. Kathryn was so smart; maybe she could think of some occupation where Susannah would be useful.

"Good morning, my pretty young ladies." Mr. Pierce came into the kitchen and poured himself a mug of coffee. "No Maria this morning?"

"She said to help yourself. There are biscuits, and I think I spied sausages in the oven."

"Danged headstrong woman. Good thing she bakes the best biscuits in the state." He filled a plate and sat down beside her.

"You don't mean that. I know she's a little gruff sometimes, but then—"

"So am I?" He laughed. "Oh, Susannah, we will sure miss you."

"You mean you don't think I've been a big bother? Melody and I weren't exactly invited guests."

He stopped chewing and turned to her. "You've

changed my whole life, girl. If I had my way, you'd never go anywhere."

She felt the blush, and her first impulse was to say she hadn't done much. But that would be against everything Nathan had made her believe in last night.

So instead of her usual denials, she only murmured, "Thank you. I'll miss you, too."

"You are welcome back here anytime. Nathan says you can't be anywhere near the ranch for at least six months or so or you'll be in terrible danger. But…"

His words just died out like he couldn't manage another sound without choking.

She reached over and took his hand. "We'll see each other again someday. I want Melody to meet you when she can remember."

"You listen to me, girl." His face was scrunched up as though he was about to explode. "You need anything. Anything. Anytime. You call me. You're my special gal, and I'll be there whenever you need me."

Oh, dear. Here came the tears again. How was she ever going to leave this place in one piece if everyone kept saying such nice things?

Darn. Darn. Darn.

Chapter 16

"You called this meeting. What did you need?" Mr. Pierce settled back into his recliner and pinned Nathan with an affirming stare.

The words and the look seemed so unlike the father he'd known since his mother died that Nathan was taken aback for a second. Everything and everyone around here had changed since Susannah and the baby arrived.

The ache in his chest grew by leaps and bounds. God, this was so hard.

"Susannah and Melody have to leave the ranch no later than tomorrow morning. Hawk says their being here will create a distraction for Samuel Grayson. It'll drive him crazy until he has to get rid of them—one way or the other. And no one wants all-out war with the Devotees."

Well, maybe *he* did. But he was too responsible for everyone else's welfare to let that happen.

"I dunno," his father began. "I wouldn't mind taking a couple of potshots at a Devotee or two." He grinned over at him, and Nathan felt closer to his old man than he had since he'd been a little kid.

He'd called this meeting for advice and maybe for a little bit of help. But learning everyone was behind him made him feel stronger already.

"Where's Derek?" His father folded his arms over his chest. "He's a part of this family, too. He should be included in this meeting."

Kathryn sat forward in her chair. "He said he'd be here. I'm sure he's just running a little late."

"And Susannah?"

"Nathan asked me to have her sit with Sara and Melody while we conduct this meeting. She and I talked about the kind of things she might like to do this morning. She's really a bright woman. Whatever we come up with, I'm sure she'll fit in fine anywhere."

"I don't like this," Mr. Pierce growled. "Not in the least. I can't stand the idea of sending such a sweet girl and her baby off into the world alone. It don't seem civilized."

You and me both, Dad. "It's not the way any of us wants things. But we have no choice."

"Why don't you go with her?"

Nathan ground his teeth with frustration. "Damn it, Dad, you know why. I have a ranch to run here."

His father muttered an unrepeatable word under his breath. "You just get stupid sometimes. You know that, boy? What's wrong with me?"

"You want to go with Susannah?"

"For pity's sake. No, I don't want to go with Susannah, but I can run this ranch—especially with Mac's help."

Nathan was about to argue the point. He'd held his negative opinions about his father's capabilities for a long time. But on second thought, maybe those opinions had always been misguided, colored by his emotions. He was seeing his father in a whole new light these days.

"I guess you probably could do a good job. But that's not the only reason I can't go."

"What else?"

"Sara. I can't leave Sara."

Kathryn leaned forward and frowned. "You think I don't do a good enough job with your niece?"

"Oh, no." Great, he was getting in deeper trouble every minute. "But Sara would never understand if I left. It's going to be hard enough to explain when Melody and Susannah disappear. But I've been the person Sara has counted on her whole life, her one constant and dependable security blanket. I can't just walk away from her."

"Maybe you won't have to." Everyone turned at the sound of Derek's voice.

His brother was lounging in the doorway with his arms crossed over his chest.

"Nice of you to show up, brother." No, no. Sarcasm was not a terrific way of getting help from your family. "Sorry, Derek. I'm a little uptight today. Did you have another idea?"

"As a matter of fact, I do. It's taken me a while to line something up. But I got confirmation this morning."

"What the hell are you talking about? We're discussing my responsibilities, mainly toward Sara. You can tell us your idea for Susannah in a moment."

"I think I've found the right answer for everyone involved, bro. You can thank me for it later."

Susannah hadn't seen Nathan all day, and the hours were slipping through her fingers. There was not enough time. But then, forever wouldn't be enough time.

Maria had come out to Sara's quarters a little while ago and told her Dr. Black had arrived and wanted to see her and the baby in her room. Maria stayed with Sara so she and Melody could go for a checkup. Hopefully the doctor would remove her stitches so at least she would be leaving the ranch with a clean slate.

She still didn't have a clue where she would be going. But Kathryn and Derek had promised they would find a good place. It felt strange, learning to rely on others for her future again after trying so hard to make things happen on her own.

But she trusted these people to help—not force her into something bad or wrong.

"Now let's take a look at that cut," Dr. Black said after he gave Melody's health a good report.

"I'm leaving tomorrow, so I sure hope you can take these stitches out today."

"Well, we'll see." He began removing the bandage. "I'm sorry to hear you're leaving. I assume you're taking the baby with you. Is that right?"

"Yes, of course." She suddenly remembered how sad he'd been on his first visit when he was looking for someone. "Did you ever find out anything about that woman and her baby you were asking about?"

"No." He still seemed sad but didn't appear to want to discuss it with her. "Well, look at that. Your skin has already knitted together. You must be a fast healer. I'll be able to remove your sutures today."

She sat still while he worked on her forehead. Finally, he stepped back and surveyed his work.

"It looks like you're going to carry a scar from this. I did the best I could, but the wound was too jagged."

She shrugged. "I'm not worried. I can start wearing bangs."

What did she care? There wouldn't be anyone around to be pretty for anyway.

The tears threatened again. She chastised herself. These waterworks had to stop. Everything was happening for a reason. And even after all he'd said, she still felt that Nathan would be better off without her in the long run. He wasn't in as deep as she was. He could find someone else someday. She knew she never would.

This was happening the way it was meant to be.

"Is she going to live, Doc?" Nathan's voice preceded him into the room.

Her heart stuttered as he appeared. It was so much easier to think of leaving when he wasn't around to remind her of all she would miss.

"Probably for a very long time," Dr. Black answered. "Unless she runs into another car explosion, that is."

"Not to worry. No explosions of any kind where she'll be going."

The doctor chuckled as he packed up his bag. "Well, good luck to you."

After the doctor left, she sat down on the edge of the bed. "What's the news? Where will I be going?"

Nathan sat down beside her and took her hand. "Before I explain, I have something to say. To ask."

His expression seemed so unfocused—not like Nathan at all.

"Okay." She couldn't imagine what was going on.

He cleared his throat. "Last night you said you loved me. Do you still feel the same way?"

Stunned, she nodded. "I…um…don't think that'll change anytime soon. But it's all right. I understand that you don't feel the same. I'll learn to live with it. Don't worry."

"Quiet," he said with a roll of his eyes. "Just listen. As it happens, I do love you—more than I ever thought possible. I was wrong not to tell you before, but I thought it would be too hard on you knowing you had to leave a man who might just perish from missing you."

"You…what?" Had she heard him right?

"I love you, Susannah Paul. And I love Melody. And I want to spend the rest of my life telling you both that. I will make you a promise. Not another day will go by that you won't know how much you are loved."

"How? On the telephone? I don't want that for you. It'll be too hard. Find someone else, Nathan—someone who can stand beside you on the ranch you love."

As much as she thrilled to hear him say the words, she hurt for him. Something that had been the hardest thing she's ever done just became impossible.

"You're not listening." He bent his head and lasered a quick kiss across her lips. "Keep that pretty mouth closed for a second. I won't be saying I love you on the telephone but in person. In bed. Every morning. And every night. I'm going with you and Melody. That is if you agree to the plan and want me."

Not want him? It would take a thousand years or more to explain how much she wanted him.

"Wait a minute." She shook her head. "What plan? What about the ranch? What about Sara?"

"My father has agreed to run the ranch until we can return. I don't expect the Devotees will be here forever. Someday they'll go. And when they do, we'll be able to come home."

She thought of Sara, how vulnerable and sweet she was. Susannah couldn't stand the thought of Sara being without Nathan. It might kill the little girl.

"But what about…?"

"Sara? Derek and Kathryn came up with an idea. I guess it was mostly Derek's plan. He's certainly surprised me."

"What's his plan?"

"Well, Kathryn's been concerned for some time that Sara wasn't getting the best treatment here on the ranch. She told Derek about some special treatments for autism that she'd read about, and he looked into them."

"But Kathryn is so good with Sara."

"Yes, she loves her—almost as much as I do. But she also knows her limitations. Out here away from civilization, Kathryn can't try any of the new treatments or medicines they've come up with in the past few years that might help Sara."

"Oh, but Sara can't leave the ranch. It's all she's ever known. What would she do without you and Kathryn?"

Nathan grinned. "You love Sara, too, don't you?"

"Certainly. Why?"

"Because Derek found a special medical center and school in the northeast where they are having miraculous results with autistic children like Sara."

"A school? With other kids?" It sounded like a dream come true for Sara.

"Yes. And wait until you hear about one of their programs. They pair the children who seem ready up with assistance dogs. The staff use canine therapy to promote socialization skills."

"Sara might love that. What a great idea."

Nathan moved in closer. "It's a great idea as long as you and I and Melody are all there to back Sara up and get her used to her new circumstances. I wouldn't want her to feel abandoned."

"No. That's not a good feeling." She knew because she'd felt that way for most of her life. "So the plan is for all of us to go? What about Kathryn?"

"I asked her to come with us to help get Sara settled." Nathan took a breath. "I thought you and I and Melody could use the extra hands—since two of us will be on our honeymoon."

"Our what?"

He took her in his arms and held her close. "It's all part of the plan," he whispered. "Marry me, Susannah. None of this will work without you. *I* won't work without you. We… I need you to make life worthwhile."

Her tears started up again. But this time she knew they were happy tears, and she could almost stand them running down her cheeks. Smiling at Nathan, she found she'd lost her voice.

"Is that a yes?"

She nodded and pulled him down for another kiss. This time she put every unsaid word behind it.

She'd been so alone for so long, and now it amazed her that she would have a whole family. More than that, Nathan had somehow made her feel like she deserved them.

Wasn't that astounding? The useless little girl she once was had broken out of her sad cocoon and turned into a butterfly. Having to leave the ranch wouldn't be an end to everything she'd grown to love, after all.

Her new life was turning into something beyond special. She was leaving the ranch much wiser than when she came and going away with the knowledge that she and her baby were loved.

She might be losing the ranch she'd come to love, but she was taking friendship and love along with her. She now had a sweet baby girl to give her life meaning and a man she loved more than life itself.

Wasn't life crazy? Running away from her old life had turned into the most magnificent new beginning she could ever have imagined.

Epilogue

Everything was set for their departure from the ranch before dawn. But no one seemed eager to leave.

The bags were in the SUV. Sara had been prepared and genuinely seemed to be looking forward to the trip. Just a second ago, Nathan had left Melody in the kitchen with his father and Maria as they took advantage of their final moments of playing with the baby. Even Mac had stopped in to say goodbye.

Derek planned on driving them to the airport in Cheyenne within the hour. But Nathan had a funny suspicion the person Derek would be most unhappy to see leave the ranch was Kathryn. Interesting, but it was a puzzle for another time.

Right now he needed to check on Susannah. Melody's things were already packed up and stowed. And Susannah couldn't have much packing to do. She barely owned any clothes—a situation he planned to remedy when they arrived in Boston.

So what was taking her so long?

Easing open the bedroom door, he stuck his head inside to see if she was dressed yet. She stood in front of the dresser, looking at herself intently in the mirror.

"What's up? You ready?"

She didn't turn, but said, "Almost all set."

When she still didn't move, he strode over to stand behind her. Checking out what she was looking at in the mirror, he saw the images of two people who were very much in love. It made him grin just to think of how happy he was that he would be standing beside this woman for life.

"What're you doing?"

"Trying to decide whether to comb my hair over my forehead or leave it back."

It was so unlike her to primp that he had to ask, "Why? What difference does it make?"

"I don't want people to be uncomfortable looking at me."

"Why would they be?"

She tsked at him. "You know. The ugly scar, silly."

He pulled her back against his chest, letting the warmth of their love surround them. "What scar? All I see is the most beautiful woman in the world."

Laughing, she pushed her hair off her forehead but then scowled at her image.

"Listen, if it really bothers you, we can consult with a plastic surgeon in Boston. I'm sure it shouldn't be any problem to fix it."

She turned away from the mirror and stepped up on her tiptoes to give him a kiss. "I love you, Nathan. If it doesn't bother you, I think I'll keep it this way."

His chest swelled with pride in her. "Okay, but why the change of heart?"

"It occurred to me that if I wanted to go back to Cold Plains now, I could. Those Devotees wouldn't want me anymore—now that I'm not perfect."

He swung her off her feet and twirled her around the room, brimming over with happiness. "Oh, but to me you are perfect, darlin'. Let's get on with our new life."

She was his wonderful love. And no matter where they lived, their lives together were bound to be absolutely perfect.

* * * * *

SUSPENSE

Heartstopping stories of intrigue and mystery—
where true love always triumphs.

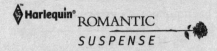

Harlequin ROMANTIC

SUSPENSE

COMING NEXT MONTH
AVAILABLE FEBRUARY 28, 2012

#1695 OPERATION MIDNIGHT
Cutter's Code
Justine Davis

#1696 A DAUGHTER'S PERFECT SECRET
Perfect, Wyoming
Kimberly Van Meter

#1697 HIGH-STAKES AFFAIR
Stealth Knights
Gail Barrett

#1698 DEADLY RECKONING
Elle James

REQUEST YOUR FREE BOOKS!
2 FREE NOVELS PLUS 2 FREE GIFTS!

◈ Harlequin®

ROMANTIC
SUSPENSE

Sparked by Danger, Fueled by Passion.

YES! Please send me 2 FREE Harlequin® Romantic Suspense novels and my 2 FREE gifts (gifts are worth about $10). After receiving them, if I don't wish to receive any more books, I can return the shipping statement marked "cancel." If I don't cancel, I will receive 4 brand-new novels every month and be billed just $4.49 per book in the U.S. or $5.24 per book in Canada. That's a saving of at least 14% off the cover price! It's quite a bargain! Shipping and handling is just 50¢ per book in the U.S. and 75¢ per book in Canada.* I understand that accepting the 2 free books and gifts places me under no obligation to buy anything. I can always return a shipment and cancel at any time. Even if I never buy another book, the two free books and gifts are mine to keep forever.

240/340 HDN FEFR

Name _____ (PLEASE PRINT)

Address _____ Apt. #

City _____ State/Prov. _____ Zip/Postal Code

Signature (if under 18, a parent or guardian must sign)

Mail to the **Reader Service:**
IN U.S.A.: P.O. Box 1867, Buffalo, NY 14240-1867
IN CANADA: P.O. Box 609, Fort Erie, Ontario L2A 5X3

Not valid for current subscribers to Harlequin Romantic Suspense books.

Want to try two free books from another line?
Call 1-800-873-8635 or visit www.ReaderService.com.

---

* Terms and prices subject to change without notice. Prices do not include applicable taxes. Sales tax applicable in N.Y. Canadian residents will be charged applicable taxes. Offer not valid in Quebec. This offer is limited to one order per household. All orders subject to credit approval. Credit or debit balances in a customer's account(s) may be offset by any other outstanding balance owed by or to the customer. Please allow 4 to 6 weeks for delivery. Offer available while quantities last.

Your Privacy—The Reader Service is committed to protecting your privacy. Our Privacy Policy is available online at www.ReaderService.com or upon request from the Reader Service.

We make a portion of our mailing list available to reputable third parties that offer products we believe may interest you. If you prefer that we not exchange your name with third parties, or if you wish to clarify or modify your communication preferences, please visit us at www.ReaderService.com/consumerschoice or write to us at Reader Service Preference Service, P.O. Box 9062, Buffalo, NY 14269. Include your complete name and address.

HRS11B

New York Times *and* USA TODAY *bestselling author*
Maya Banks presents book three in her miniseries
PREGNANCY & PASSION.

TEMPTED BY HER INNOCENT KISS

Available March 2012 from Harlequin Desire!

There came a time in a man's life when he knew he was well and truly caught. Devon Carter stared down at the diamond ring nestled in velvet and acknowledged that this was one such time. He snapped the lid closed and shoved the box into the breast pocket of his suit.

He had two choices. He could marry Ashley Copeland and fulfill his goal of merging his company with Copeland Hotels, thus creating the largest, most exclusive line of resorts in the world, or he could refuse and lose it all.

Put in that light, there wasn't much he could do except pop the question.

The doorman to his Manhattan high-rise apartment hurried to open the door as Devon strode toward the street. He took a deep breath before ducking into his car, and the driver pulled into traffic.

Tonight was the night. All of his careful wooing, the countless dinners, kisses that started brief and casual and became more breathless—all a lead-up to tonight. Tonight his seduction of Ashley Copeland would be complete, and then he'd ask her to marry him.

He shook his head as the absurdity of the situation hit him for the hundredth time. Personally, he thought William Copeland was crazy for forcing his daughter down Devon's throat.

Ashley was a sweet enough girl, but Devon had no desire

to marry anyone.

William had other plans. He'd told Devon that Ashley had no head for the family business. She was too softhearted, too naive. So he'd made Ashley part of the deal. The catch? Ashley wasn't to know of it. Which meant Devon was stuck playing stupid games.

Ashley was supposed to think this was a grand love match. She was a starry-eyed woman who preferred her animal-rescue foundation over board meetings, charts and financials for Copeland Hotels.

If she ever found out the truth, she wouldn't take it well.

And hell, he couldn't blame her.

But no matter the reason for his proposal, before the night was over, she'd have no doubts that she belonged to him.

What will happen when Devon marries Ashley?
Find out in Maya Banks's passionate new novel
TEMPTED BY HER INNOCENT KISS
Available March 2012 from Harlequin Desire!

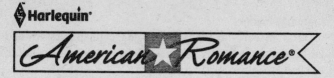

Harlequin®

American ★ Romance®

Get swept away with author

CATHY GILLEN THACKER

and her new miniseries

Legends of Laramie County

On the Cartwright ranch, it's the women
who endure and run the ranch—and it's time for
lawyer Liz Cartwright to take over. Needing some help
around the ranch, Liz hires Travis Anderson, a fellow
attorney, and Liz's high-school boyfriend. Travis says
he wants to get back to his ranch roots, but Liz knows
Travis is running from something. Old feelings emerge
as they work together, but Liz can't help but wonder
if Travis is home to stay.

Reluctant Texas Rancher

**Available March
wherever books are sold.**

www.Harlequin.com

HAR75398